MASON put his hand up and touched my hair. Then he brought his hand around my shoulder and slowly down my back. He held it there, hesitantly, as though he didn't know what to do next. I didn't know what I should do either. But I decided to do what I felt like doing and put my arms around his neck. We were so close, I could hear his heart thumping. Maybe he could hear mine, too. We were both sort of out of breath.

"I guess you should go in," he said breathlessly, like he didn't want me to.

"I guess." I didn't want to, either, but I was a little scared of what might happen next if I didn't. I used to read about people getting "carried away," but I never knew what it meant before.

"I'll call you tomorrow," he said softly, as I went into the house, walking on air.

The Queen

of the

What Ifs

Norma Klein

FAWCETT JUNIPER • NEW YORK

The author and publisher are grateful to Jennifer Fleissner for permission to reprint her poems "From Tracy with Love" and "For Robin."

A Fawcett Juniper Book
Published by Ballantine Books
Copyright © 1982 by Norma Klein

ISBN 0-449-70026-7

Manufactured in the United States of America

First Fawcett Juniper Edition: June 1982
First Ballantine Books Edition: July 1982
Fourth Printing: November 1984

One

I'M NOT superstitious. I'm still not, even though it started on Friday the thirteenth. One reason for that is that I was born on Friday the thirteenth so I can't very well regard that as an unlucky day! Even though horoscopes never seem to say things that come true, that doesn't stop me from reading them the next time around and even believing them, especially if they say I'm going to make a lot of money or that someone is going to fall madly in love with me.

We were driving to the airport to pick up my older sister, Vanessa, who's just finished her first year of college. "We" is Mom, Dad, Lowell and I. Lowell is my older brother; he's seventeen. He's not really *that* much older, only a year and two months. I used to have the feeling maybe I wasn't planned since you'd wonder how many couples would want to have a third child a year after they had their second, especially if they had a boy and a girl already. Mom says no, they just liked kids and figured while they were at it, another might be a good idea. "We were just babies," she says, "what did we know?" I've never felt unwanted or anything, but I think when I'm a mother I'll take it a bit more slowly.

The good thing about Lowell and me being so near in age is that we're really close, much more so than most brothers and sisters I know. I've always looked up to Vanessa, but four years is a big gap, especially when you're little. If I have a problem or just want to talk to someone about something, I always go to Lowell. He's a really good listener. He sits there, looking at you with his brownish green eyes (he wears glasses), sometimes saying "Umm hmm" or "Yeah, I know" but in this very understanding way. Talking to my best friend, Terry, is completely different. She's always gasping, "Oh my God, no! You *didn't*!" or "How fantastic! I can't *believe* it!" Once when we were in a coffee shop talking about something, she got up to go to the bathroom and said, "Now listen, don't say a *word* till I get back." As though there was anyone for me to say anything *to,* since I was there just with her.

Our car is a station wagon. I guess most people who live in the suburbs—we live in Rockland County, which is about half an hour from New York—still have big cars. Sometimes, like this time, Lowell and I lie down in the "way back"—that's the name we thought up for it—where the luggage would go if we were carrying luggage. There's a nice, soft blanket there and a pillow and some books and magazines. You can lie in any position you want. Usually Mom and Dad sit in the front and talk or listen to music—there's a hi-fi in the front. This time, though, we were lying there, each thinking our own thoughts, when suddenly Mom practically yelled from the front seat, "Because it's shit, that's why!"

I should explain that Mom, in general, goes off like a firecracker when she's mad, whereas Dad tends to be more measured and quiet. Still, she doesn't often go around screaming "Because it's shit!" quite that loud or that vehemently, so I kind of started and looked up.

"You'll get a job eventually if you'll just be patient," Dad said in his calm voice.

"How?" Mom yelled, or maybe she wasn't yelling throughout the whole conversation, just talking in a very loud voice. "Will you please tell me how someone who has never had a *single* job, not even a high school job, who has wasted fifteen years painting pictures no one will buy...who is going to offer such a person a job? Please tell me!"

"Someone will," Dad said softly.

"You just don't know what it's like," Mom said.

"I do know," Dad said.

"You don't," Mom insisted. "You don't know because you've never been through it. You don't know what it's like to go through these horrible humiliating job interviews and have people half your age sneer at you. You don't *know*! Because you have a comfortable, well-paying job that you like and you're good at. It's so far removed from anything you've ever had to go through, you can't even empathize or——"

"Darling, I can," Dad said. "Will you believe me when I say I can?"

"No!" Mom said.

Dad glanced nervously at us; we were at a stop sign. "How are you doing, kids?" he said.

"Okay," Lowell said.

"Don't let our argument bother you," he said. "It's nothing important, okay?"

"Nothing important?" Mom yelled. That time she really *did* yell. "My *life* is not important?"

"Hope, you have *got* to calm down," Dad said.

"*Why* have I got to?"

"Because I can't drive with all this tension. I've had a long, hard day and I just can't take it, that's all."

"*I'll* drive," Mom said.

"Can't we just discuss this later?" Dad said.

"No," Mom said. "Because it's always later and the truth is you don't give a damn and don't want to discuss it, *ever*. So it's always later, later, later."

"Daddy," I said, "I think I feel a little bit carsick."

"You see," Dad said, sounding angry.

"Will you stop that?" Mom said. "She *always* gets carsick. Stop trying to make me feel guilty!"

Dad pulled the car over to a roadside place. Mom got out and stalked off the the Ladies' Room. I'd thought I was going to throw up but once I got outside, I felt better. Dad, Lowell and I stood there in silence.

"How do you feel now, hon?" Dad asked.

"Better," I said.

"I'm sorry about this," he said. "Mom is just very upset."

"We gathered that," Lowell said.

"It's all going to work out," Dad said. "But right now it's difficult." He sighed and ran his fingers through his hair.

Dad is handsome. I don't know how to describe him exactly. He looks a little like Kris Kristofferson only without a beard and not so hippie-ish looking. In fact, he's not hippie-ish looking at all. But he has dark blond hair and he's thin. Usually he has a kind of worried, thoughtful expression, like something is bothering him that he can't figure out. Sometimes he looks relaxed—when he's playing the piano or throwing the frisbee at us on some summer evening. But most of the time he looks worried.

Mom is sort of funny looking. She has bright red hair—orangy red—which I guess is odd for someone who's Jewish. She has big brown eyes and a lot of freckles that get worse in the summer. Her clothes are peculiar. Mostly she wears jeans and odd T-shirts—like the one she had on today, which had a broken egg being cracked in the middle. She also has one that says, "You're Not Getting Older, You're Getting Better," and one with a great big eye right in the middle. She's not exactly chic. When they go out in the evening, Dad usually looks really good in some kind of suit and tie, and Mom looks kind of strange. Once she gets out of her jeans, she doesn't know what to wear. She's said that herself. She has this one party dress that has zigzag stripes going all around it in a million colors. It's nice, only she's had it for about a hundred years so it's not that new looking anymore. She says she can't find anything she really likes. Once she said she wanted to be buried in that dress unless she finds one she likes more.

Mom came out of the Ladies' Room looking like she'd washed her face and brushed her hair. Her hair is wild and curly looking, but when she brushes it, it can settle down a bit. When she gets mad, her cheeks turn bright pink, like someone in a cartoon, but now they looked regular again. She didn't say a word in the car until we drove up to the bus where Vanessa was waiting.

Vanessa was sitting cross-legged on the ground with her duffle bag and stuff around her. When she saw us, she jumped up and began waving. She ran over, dragging her gear behind her.

"Hey, you're half an hour late," she said. "How come?"

"We had a problem on the road," Dad said. He got out and hugged her. She leaned in the window and kissed Mom.

"You look great," Mom said. She admires Vanessa a lot. She says she wishes she'd had Vanessa's drive and energy when she was that age.

Vanessa got in the middle seat. "Hi, kids," she said to us.

I don't think she meant to be condescending. It's just we probably still strike her as "kids," even though we feel grown up compared to the way we used to be.

"Well, at least I got to write a poem while I was waiting for you guys," she said.

"You did?" Mom said. "Where?"

"Oh, I did it in the margin of this magazine." She waved a crumpled copy of *Ms.* "Want to hear it?"

"Sure," Dad said, starting up the car.

Vanessa is always writing poems. She's been doing it since she was six years old! She'll be just sitting there at the table, eating a sandwich, and all of a sudden she'll rush off and half an hour later she'll poke this poem in your face and say, "Tell me what you think." This year that she's been away at college, all the letters she's written home have been poems. The ones to me start out "Dear Robin" (that's my name), then the poem, then, "Love, V." That's all! No news about what she's doing or her friends or her grades.

It's a little hard on me, going to the same high school Vanessa went to. Even though I'm four years younger, I have a lot of the same teachers she did, and they all remember her. I think even if it were ten years later, they'd remember her. Not all of them liked her, but she's the kind of person people remember. Our English teacher, Mr. Karasik, says Vanessa was the best student he's ever had or ever hopes to have. Once he wrote on one of her papers, "Having you as a student makes my life worthwhile."

Vanessa's not exactly pretty—she has a big nose and dark brown eyes like Mom—but when she reads her poems in public, you don't notice anyone but her. Her eyes gleam and she tosses her hair back and her voice goes from soft and throaty to almost a yell. Now, sitting in the middle seat, she turned so we could all hear her and read us the poem she'd written while she was waiting for us.

"It's about Tracy Austin," she said. "You know, the tennis player?"

The sun rises for me
Differently than for any other.
My days rank star sapphire
On the jewel-tipped scale
That measures human fortune.
I've been called lucky;
For me, the word has a different connotation.

Spending my days
Divided from the world
By a net
Getting Avon makeovers
From the star-struck employees
Of my own empire.

Nights wasted at fourteen
Sipping leathery gin
From a mug inscribed with my signature
That is currently selling for $49.99
At Bloomie's.

The yellow moon
Glows down at me
Like an angry young tennis ball.
Lifting my racket
I serve
The sky.

I didn't want to say anything first because
I'm never sure I understand Vanessa's poems.

But Dad said, "Hey, I love that last image! 'I serve the sky.'" Dad used to write a lot in college and still does, on weekends and stuff. He's the one Vanessa usually shows her poems to first.

"It's good they have yellow tennis balls now," Lowell commented. "If they were white, you'd be in trouble."

"Moons are white as much as yellow," I pointed out.

Mom turned around. "You're kind of down on this poor kid, aren't you?" she said. "What did she do that was so bad? Be successful?"

"She's sold out is what V means," Dad said. "She's taken her talent and exploited it."

"Better exploit it than let it rot," Mom said.

I was afraid they were going to get into an argument again. I knew Mom was thinking of herself, that she'd let her talent for art go to waste. But Vanessa just said airily, "She's just a symbol, Mom."

"Leathery gin is good," Dad chuckled. "I don't know if I've ever had any leathery gin, but I know what you mean."

There was a moment of silence. "Are you going to try and get it published?" I asked. Vanessa has sent some of her poems to magazines, like *Seventeen,* but so far they've just written nice notes. Dad says all writers have to start that way.

"I have to work on it," Vanessa said. "Did I tell you I have this really terrific writing teacher this year? Steve Brody?"

"Sounds like a football player," Dad said.

"He's super!" Vanessa said, leaning forward enthusiastically. "I've learned more in the last four months than in all of high school. I mean, Karasik was a sweetie, but Steve knows so much! He might come to New York, he said, and I told him he could stay with us—is that okay?"

The college Vanessa goes to isn't that well known—it's called Buckshire—but she picked it over lots of other famous places where she was accepted, like Yale and Smith, because you can design your own courses. It's especially for students who are very "inner motivated." I don't think I am inner motivated. If I didn't get good grades for college, I don't know if I'd bother studying that much, except at things I really like, like music.

I've been studying the cello for seven years, since I was eight, and I think I'll do something professionally with music when I'm older. But music isn't for me what poetry is for Vanessa. She's never wanted to do anything *but* that since she was born, practically. She says she might get a job to earn money, but if people ask her what she is, she always says, "A poet," in a very firm, no-doubt-about-it way, whereas I can imagine doing something totally different from music—becoming an anthropologist, say, and going off on digs. Or maybe Terry and I will become lawyers and start our own law firm.

We'll only take on really terrible cases, people who can't get anyone else to represent them. Dad is always saying, "Keep your options open." That's what I want to do.

Two

THAT NIGHT Vanessa's two best friends, Cooper and Wendy, came over for dinner. One unusual thing about Vanessa is that she's always had best friends who were boys as well as some who were girls. I've only had girls for best friends, unless you count Lowell—and I don't think you can because he's my brother. Vanessa's a really strong feminist, but she says she thinks it's dumb that she's supposed to regard all women as sisters. She says she thinks some women are total fools and lots of men are really great, and she refuses to have her social life pigeonholed that way. Not that anyone *could* pigeonhole her, even if they tried, she's so strong-minded.

Dinner was okay. I still felt nervous thinking about the argument Mom and Dad had in the car, but they seemed pretty normal once we got home. Mom made leg of lamb, Vanessa's favorite, and there were little peas with onions and rice. For dessert Dad made his specialty, a German apple pancake which is gigantic. You eat it with jam and powdered sugar; it's really good.

"So, what's with your name, Mom?" Vanessa asked, reaching for another slice of pancake. "Are you a Vey or a Herskowitz?"

"A who or a what?" Cooper said.

"Mom's maiden name is Herskowitz," Vanessa explained, "and if she were getting married now she'd never change it because no one does anymore."

"*No* one does anymore?" Dad interjected, but Vanessa didn't seem to hear him. She rushed on.

"So, she was thinking maybe she'd go back legally to Herskowitz now that she's getting a job, and we could all choose what we wanted to be. My problem is that Vanessa Vey is just a better writing name, don't you think?"

"How about Oy?" Cooper said. "Then you could be Oy Vey."

Vanessa socked him. "No, seriously, I don't know what to do."

"You could hyphenate it," Wendy suggested.

"Vey-Herskowitz?" Vanessa said. "That sounds weird."

"*I'd* consider Herskowitz," Lowell said. I knew he was saying that to make Mom feel better. Personally, I don't think either name is that great and I'm not going to be a writer, but Robin Vey is, at least, short. And I know this girl named Shirley Herskowitz whom I can't stand. That's not Mom's fault, but I can't help associating the name with her. Also, I just think of myself as Robin Vey since that's who I've been for fifteen years.

"Actually, hon," Mom said, "I don't think I'm going to bother legally changing it."

"Why not?" Vanessa said indignantly. "It's a great idea."

"Well." Mom looked away. "I talked to a lawyer and he said it's a big complicated thing. He said I should just use Herskowitz once I start working, if ever."

"But that's a cop-out," Vanessa exclaimed. "What lawyer *was* that? He sounds like some sexist idiot."

"It was Ogden Haynes," Mom said, "and he's definitely *not* a sexist idiot."

Vanessa narrowed her eyes. "Are you sure?"

"He's just an idiot, period," Dad said.

Mom turned red. "In what way? Ogden's a sensitive, lovely person."

"His wife treated him like a laughingstock," Dad said curtly. "And he just sat there and took it."

Ogden Haynes' wife was this woman named Priscilla who left him a few years ago. He has this really cute son Mason who used to be in our school, but he transferred a year ago.

"In what way a laughingstock?" Mom said, standing up. I could see she was getting angry again. "She was going out of her mind and she needed to get away. The fact that he's accepted it, understood it, coped—*that* makes him a laughingstock?"

Dad cleared his throat. "Any more pancakes, anyone?" he said, looking around the table.

I looked at Lowell. I was beginning to feel funny again.

"Hey, Vey!" Cooper said, getting up. "Are we going to that movie or what?"

"Listen, someone with a tag like Cooper Kaufman is not exactly in a position to sneer," Vanessa said, but good-naturedly.

"Cooper Kaufman collected kvetchy cuties," Cooper said. "Do I have the makings of a poet or don't I?"

"Kvetchy cooties?" Wendy said.

After they left, I helped stack the dishes in the dishwasher. Dad went into his study and Mom said she was going to take a walk. I went into the den to watch a movie on TV. Now that school's over, I can stay up as late as I want, but I usually get tired around eleven anyway. In one of the commercial breaks, I decided to get a snack. As I came near the kitchen, I heard Mom and Dad. They were having another fight.

The house was absolutely still, and I could hear their voices as though they were in the same room with me.

"Fine," Mom was saying. "If that's what you want to do—run out on the whole thing—fine. Go with my blessing."

"I'm not running out," Dad said. "I'm going because I have to preserve my sanity, okay? I simply can't take this anymore."

"Okay, terrific," Mom said. "You just go and I'll cope with the kids and the house and everything else."

"The kids will be busy with their jobs and are old enough to look after themselves. That's one reason now seemed like a good time to me," Dad said.

"It's a perfect time," Mom said. "It's a wonderful time."

"Look, Leo said I could have his place. I feel like I want to try and finish my novel. I just need some peace and quiet for two months. Is that asking so much?"

"Go and finish your damn novel!" Mom bellowed. "And go fuck Helen Becker, if that's what you want. I don't give a damn."

"This has nothing to do with Helen Becker," Dad said.

"Bullshit!" Mom said. "God, if there is one thing I cannot stand about men, it is their total and absolute dishonesty."

"I never slept with her," Dad said. "I swear."

"So, within a month you will," Mom said.

"And you'll have a nice, quiet, comfortable place to do it in."

"You want to make it seem like this has to do with her and it doesn't."

"What *does* it have to do with, then?" Mom said.

"It has to do with the fact that you are in a perpetually ferocious mood about things which are *not* my fault. It is *not* my fault you never got a job and can't get one now. You're blaming me for things that have nothing to do with me. And I don't like it. It's not pleasant to live with, okay?"

"So, go where it's pleasant," Mom said, her voice shaking. "Go where you'll have someone to sit around massaging your ego and telling you how terrific you are. If you're *that* weak, if that's what you need, then go!"

"I will," Dad said in this very cold, flat voice.

"When?"

"Tomorrow."

I crept back upstairs and knocked on Lowell's door.

"Lowell?"

"Yeah?"

"Can I come in?"

"Sure."

Lowell was reading in bed. His room, unlike mine, is very neat and spare looking. I sat down on the floor next to his bed.

"Listen, something awful is happening," I said.

"What?"

"It's Mom and Dad...they had a terrible fight again."

"About what?"

"He's going to live in the city over the summer and Mom thinks he's going to have an affair with Helen Becker."

"Helen Becker?" Lowell looked surprised. Helen Becker is someone who works in Dad's architectural firm. She's divorced and has a daughter about two years younger than I am whom I don't like that much. I guess Mrs. Becker is pretty. She's tall and thin and has curly blond hair and big glasses and she paints her fingernails. She's the only person I ever met who does that. They're quite long and usually pink or sometimes red.

"What if they get divorced?" I said anxiously.

"Rob, don't jump the gun...it's only for two months."

"Yeah, but what if he *does* have an affair with Helen Becker and decides he wants to marry her?"

"He's got more sense than that."

"What if Mom gets so mad at him for doing it she won't let him come back?"

"You know what you are?" Lowell said, amused. "The queen of the what ifs."

"Aren't you scared, though? I *hate* it when they fight! I *hate* it!"

"I wish Mom could get a job," Lowell said thoughtfully. "I feel bad about that."

"Do you think it would make all the difference?"

"I think it would help. She seems to care about it so much."

"Maybe she will," I said. I looked at Lowell. "He's going tomorrow."

"So soon?"

"Yeah. His friend, Leo, is lending him an apartment."

Lowell looked thoughtful. "At least we'll be around.... That'll make Mom feel better."

Lowell has a job at our local library four days a week from noon to five. I'm supposed to tutor some kids in cello at the Rockland Music Center. I take lessons there myself, but my teacher, Joanie Molina, said she thought it would be good experience for me to give lessons. She said most musicians have to teach to earn a living since there just aren't that many jobs in orchestras or chamber music groups. What I'd really like to do when I'm out of college is what Joanie is doing now: she and these three friends are forming their own string quartet. It's all women; they went to the same music school together. Joanie says it's really hard and the chances of making it are small, but they're going to give it their best effort. They're doing some recording over the summer; that's one reason she'll be away.

I was sort of looking forward to the summer, but I'd imagined it completely differently. I'd imagined Dad would be around and he'd play tennis with me and Lowell, the way he usually does. I don't get much exercise over the winter, and I think I could get good at tennis if I practiced more. Not good like Tracy Austin, but good enough to maybe beat Lowell. Right now we're about even. His serve is better, but my shots go in more of the time when we're rallying.

This is the first summer ever that Terry hasn't been here. I think Mom is glad. She said that last summer all Terry and I did was lie in my room and listen to records. That isn't true. It may have seemed like that, but we were actually planning a lot of important things, like a magazine we may be starting. When school is on, we're too busy to talk that much, except on weekends. But this summer Terry went to France with a group called "The Experiment in International Living." She'll live with a French family for a month and then bicycle somewhere in France the next month. She said I shouldn't take it personally if she didn't write much. Terry hates writing. She usually gets *C*'s in English, even from Ms. Beckman who gives everyone grades that are much higher than they deserve. I hope I can manage without her.

"Lowell, can I stay in here for a while?" I asked him.

"Sure," Lowell said.

I got a copy of *Rolling Stone* from my room and sat in Lowell's bean-bag chair leafing through it. Being in Lowell's room is very peaceful. It's the neatest room you'll ever see. Dad says there's a group in interior design that believes only things that are functional are beautiful. Lowell must feel that way too because he doesn't have stacks of old junk lying in heaps all over the place like me. He just has what he needs and not a thing more. Another reason it's peaceful to be with him is that whatever he's doing, Lowell concentrates a hundred percent. He's not like me, sitting here leafing through *Rolling Stone* but thinking about a million other things. Lowell wants to be an engineer when he grows up, the kind who designs bridges and things. Some people's bridges I would not want to go over, but Lowell's I definitely will. He won't design one unless everything about it is figured out perfectly.

Gradually I began to feel sleepy. "I guess I'll turn in now," I said. "Thanks." I hurried back to my room and got into bed before I had a chance to let that good feeling go away.

Three

VANESSA'S ATTITUDE about Dad's moving into the city was completely different. "I think it's a terrific idea," she said. The two of us were in the kitchen. Everyone else was out.

"In what way?" I said.

"Look, he's been talking about finishing his novel for nine million years. He needs to get away, off by himself, without any distractions. I can understand that perfectly."

"You don't think it's an excuse?"

Vanessa grabbed another honey bun. It was

breakfast for her; she'd gotten up at eleven. "Writing's not an excuse," she said. "He's bored with his job. He needs to feel really tuned in to something."

"But how about Mom?"

"Mom can manage....Rob, marriage isn't two people *chained* together for life. It's two people living and doing things alone, together, whatever. Whatever works....All that stuff is crap, that togetherness, suburban thing. It was just a media hype."

"Yeah?" Vanessa is so definite about everything. I wish I could be like that. What I really wanted to ask her about was Helen Becker, but I had to go off to give my first lesson.

When I got back, Dad had already left. But he called that evening. I answered the phone.

"Rob," he said. "Listen, I'm sorry I didn't have a chance to say good-bye before I took off this afternoon."

"Oh, that's okay," I said.

"You and Lowell could just jump on the bus some afternoon and come down to see me. It's only half an hour."

"Sure," I said. "We'd like to."

"There's a lot of good restaurants around here," he went on. "There's a Japanese one down the block that looks intriguing....When is Lowell's day off? Friday?"

"Yeah, only I have a lesson to give in the morning....I could do it in the afternoon though."

"How're they going? Did you start yet?"

"I just had two. One's this little kid, around seven? So it's hard to tell....But this other girl is fantastic. She just started a year ago and she's already doing Bach's études."

"Do you like it, though? Teaching?"

"Yeah, I think so."

I know Dad thinks teaching can get too routine and boring after a while, but I think that would be after years of doing it, not after just one day. And maybe now that he's bored with his job, he thinks of everything in terms of how boring it might turn out to be if you chose it as a profession.

"Are you going to have enough to do?" Dad said. Maybe he was feeling guilty about leaving; I don't know.

"Well, Lowell and I are going to play tennis twice a week," I said.

"Good....You know, we can play in the city too....There are public courts up here. I just meant—well, I'll be here and Hope is going to spend a lot of time commuting to her classes at Parsons. I don't want you two to feel too...well, abandoned or whatever."

"Oh, no," I said, laughing as though that were the dumbest idea ever. "We'll be fine."

"The point is," Dad said, "I'm right over the bridge. Just pick up the phone and call me whenever you feel like it. I'll be just sitting here most of the time, crumpling papers up and tossing them into the wastebasket."

I felt better. Maybe that's all he *will* be doing. Maybe Helen Becker is on vacation in Paris or somewhere far away for two months! I hope so.

No one but Lowell knows I heard Mom and Dad have that fight, even Mom. She thinks we believe what they told us—that Dad just needs time to work on his novel. I guess people think kids are easily fooled.

After I hung up, I went back to my room. I had a kind of stomachache from talking to Dad. If only he *would* just finish his novel and not have an affair with Helen Becker! And if only Mom would get a good job and stop screaming and start acting nice to him again! Oh, I just pray that happens. I *pray* they don't get divorced.

Mom poked her head in the door. "Hon, I think we're going to go out to the Szechuan Palace. I'm not up to cooking. Okay?"

The four of us—me, Lowell, Vanessa and Mom—had dinner together. In a way it's easier if you're just four. More tables are built to fit four people. When Dad is there, they have to move an extra table over that would usually seat six. But I wished he was there, even if we would have had to wait longer for a table.

Vanessa was all excited because a friend of Cooper's thinks he can get her a job as a waitress in a Greenwich Village coffee house. He said she can make a lot on tips. Also, at night writers, especially poets, sometimes read from their works there. Of course, most of them are published poets, but Vanessa thinks maybe she can convince the owner of the place to let her read.

"Sounds like a great idea," Mom said, but in a sad, dreamy kind of way as if she wasn't completely paying attention.

"Of course I haven't even gotten the job," Vanessa said, "but I think I can. He said the owner likes arty, intense types. So, isn't that me?"

"Definitely," Lowell said.

"I'll just go heavy on the eye makeup and wrap my hair languorously around my neck." Vanessa smiled mischievously.

We began looking at the menu. Then we ordered. But it was a little like Mom wasn't quite there. She didn't talk much, the way she usually does.

"I'm glad you're having the winter melon soup," Lowell said to her, as though he wanted to draw her into the conversation.

"Umm," Mom said.

"How come they have winter melon if it's summer?" I asked.

"It's just a name," Lowell said. He never makes you feel stupid if you don't know something.

"Hey, isn't that Ogden Haynes over there?" Vanessa said.

At that Mom, who had been staring sort of morosely at nothing and smoking (even though she supposedly gave it up years ago), perked up and said, "Oh, damn...yes. I guess I'll have to tell him about Joel."

I saw that Ogden Haynes' son, Mason, was sitting next to him. I am really awful with boys! Mason used to be in the school orchestra with me—he played the clarinet—and I had the vague feeling he liked me. He'd come up to me after rehearsals and make desultory conversation, kind of pawing the ground and looking at me sideways. He's one of those boys who has incredibly long, beautiful eyelashes, the kind girls are supposed to have. Anyhow, if I'd been Terry I would have bubbled on and made engaging small talk and wheedled him into asking me out, but being me, I just pawed the ground and looked at *him* sideways. That went on for about a year and then he transferred to this all-boys prep school and I haven't seen him since. I hate to say it, but that's sort of typical of my social life thus far.

The waiter brought the soup and Lowell served us. "Eat up, Mom, come on," he said.

Mom was just sitting there, fiddling with her chopsticks. "Yeah, sure," she said. "It's good, isn't it?"

"She doesn't feel that hungry," I said.

"So, Ogden Haynes knows or doesn't know," Vanessa said. "Who cares?" Vanessa never seems to care what people think, or maybe she doesn't even notice, I'm not sure. I'm more like Mom, I do care, even if I think it's dumb.

"He might not even see us," I said nervously, but I could see Mason was looking at me.

"I thought you liked Ogden Haynes," Lowell said, puzzled. "So what if—"

"Kids, come on," Mom said. "He might hear us—he's right over there."

"What's to hear?" Vanessa said, spooning up more soup.

"It's not that I care what Ogden thinks," Mom said defensively. "Why should I?"

There was a pause.

"Grandma says there's a great new Chinese restaurant near here," I said, just to shift the topic slightly.

"I read about that in the *New York Times*," Lowell said.

Lowell reads about *everything* in the *New York Times*. That's one way we're completely different. I only like to read things that are made up and Lowell only likes to read things that are true. Mainly he reads history books and books on science. He read all of Shirer's *The Rise and Fall of the Third Reich* this year and now he's into Carl Sagan's *Cosmos*. When you see Lowell sitting there in his bean-bag chair, reading, you can tell he's practically humming with pleasure. Facts just turn him on. He gets this expression like a cat lying in the sun when he's reading some new facts. Whereas I can see the *point* of them, but they don't turn me on. The only science I ever liked was geology, because dinosaurs, even though they were real, don't *seem* real. I love dinosaurs. I used to go with Lowell to the Museum of Natural History when we'd go to the city to visit Grandma. He would tell me all these facts and I would not really listen, but we'd both have a good time.

Lowell had ordered sea bass with mushrooms. He has a rule that he always orders something new each time we go out to eat. He thinks it's terrible to do what I do, order the same thing— lobster Cantonese or sweet-and-sour pork— time and again. But I know I'm going to like them and with new things you never know. Lowell says it's important to expand your taste horizons. Maybe he's right.

While we were all accepting lumps of Lowell's bass, Ogden Haynes walked by our table. Seeing us, he stopped and said, "Hi, folks."

"Hi, Ogden," Mom said. She lit up another cigarette so I knew she was nervous again.

"I haven't seen you folks lately," he said. "Where's Joel?"

"Joel just moved to New York," Mom said through a cloud of smoke.

"New York?" Ogden Haynes said, as though she'd said Timbuktu.

"Yeah, New York. His address is 420 Riverside Drive, if you want to get in touch with him."

"Oh," said Ogden Haynes. Frankly, I don't think he probably *did* especially want to get in touch with Dad—why should he?—but maybe Mom thought that since he works in New York, they might want to have lunch together. "That would be nice," he said.

"It's just for the summer," Mom said, talking very fast. "He's trying to finish his novel and a friend of ours lent him an apartment."

"That sounds great," said Ogden Haynes. He looked even more basset-houndish and ill at ease than usual. "Well, see you around, then."

Terry used to call Ogden Haynes the "Incredible Hulk Squared." He's six feet four with very broad shoulders, but what's odd is that he has very small eyes and an extremely soft voice, like they belonged to another person. She saw him at our house because Mom and Dad used to go out with him and his wife before his wife left him. Also, he's handled things like their will for them. Mason is tall too, but in not such a hulkish way, just solid.

When he was out of earshot, Mom sighed and said, "One down. Nine hundred to go...maybe I ought to make that into a cassette and just play it when anyone asks me."

"So, someone asks you," Vanessa said. "What's so bad about that?"

"Nothing," Mom said. "I just don't like lying."

"It's not a lie....Dad *did* go to New York and he *is* going to try and finish his novel," Vanessa said. "Isn't he?"

I kicked Lowell under the table; I didn't dare look at him.

Mom said, "He went to New York. I haven't the foggiest notion if he'll ever come back. He did *not* go to finish his novel. He went to get away from me and to screw around with any friendly, kind soul he can find who will listen to his tale of woe about his awful, hysterical wife....Would *that* make a good cassette?"

"Mom, I don't know," Vanessa said in her low, soothing voice. "That sounds a little exaggerated."

"It's an exaggeration of the *truth*," Mom said.

"Why do you assume he's going to screw around? He's not like that."

"Everyone is like that," Mom said.

Lowell shook his head. "Dad loves you....I don't get it."

"Listen, kids," Mom said, pointing her finger at us. "Let me tell you a few things....Joel and I married because we were in love: correct. But after twenty-odd years, and I underline *odd*, a lot of water has flowed under the bridge."

"Meaning?" Vanessa said.

"Meaning people make choices and then are disappointed with those choices."

"Which choices?" I said. "Who is disappointed with what choices?"

"Dad is disappointed," Mom said, "because he doesn't have a nice, bouncy, cheerful wife who's earning thirty thousand a year and has it all together like...Helen Becker."

"Oh, Helen Becker's a fool," Vanessa said.

Mom looked pleased to hear her say that. "Or Sallie Snyder or Nancy Spinelli...or anyone you can name."

"I don't believe Dad cares that much that you aren't earning anything," Lowell said. "*You* care. He doesn't."

"Okay, touché. He cares partly because I care. That's true."

"I don't see *why* you care so much," Vanessa said.

"I'll tell you why," Mom said. "I care because twenty years ago I was the best damn student in the art department at Cornell, because everyone predicted great things for me, because I predicted great things for myself and because I have done *nothing*, nothing at all."

"How about us?" Lowell said wryly.

"Okay, you.... You're terrific, all of you. You're the best thing I ever did. But...you're growing up and out. And what am I left with?"

"But you'll get a job eventually, Mom," I said.

"I'll get a job, if I'm lucky, at ten thousand a year, with a boss who's twenty-seven. And I'll do shit work for ten years and no one will give a damn that I was once so wonderful they didn't know what to do because I won all the prizes they gave out."

"Well," Lowell said. "That's life."

Mom gave him a dirty glance. "Is it ever. And till they think up a good substitute, it's what we're stuck with."

"I'm sorry," Vanessa said seriously, putting her hand on Mom's. "I really am, Mom."

"Me too," Lowell piped up.

Mom looked like she was going to cry.

"Dad'll come back," I said hopefully. "I don't think he even likes Helen Becker that much."

"Oh, Helen Becker is a symbol," Mom said. "If it's not Helen Becker, it's someone else.... The woods are full of hungry females."

Vanessa smiled. "Listen, Dad can defend himself."

"Who says he wants to?" said Mom.

Back at the house, I didn't feel like going back to my room. I decided to go in and pester Lowell again. He was reading, as usual.

"I feel nervous," I said.

"Take a hot bath."

"What do you think's going to happen?"

"About what?"

"About them, dodo!"

"How should I know? He'll come home in August, like he said."

"But what if——"

"Rob, maybe he really just wants to finish his novel."

Dad's been working on this novel since practically before we were born from what I gather. He won't let anyone see it, even Mom. Every summer he says this is the one he's going to finish it. He goes into his study where he has millions of index cards, all filed under subjects and subheadings. If he sees anything in a newspaper or magazine that might go in the novel, he clips it out and files it away. I don't actually know how much real writing he's done so far. When I pass the study, I can hear the typewriter clicking away, so he must have done something.

In college Dad used to write stories. He said he was just like Vanessa. He'd be sitting around and an idea would hit him and he'd run off and stay up all night writing it. Some of them were published in the college literary magazine, *The Heron,* and we have copies down in the basement. But I guess once he went to architectural school, he didn't have much time to write.

It's funny that Dad is so bored with being an architect because so many people seem to think it sounds like a wonderful thing to be. Dad says that's because they imagine it's a perfect fusion of art and utility, but now with inflation nobody can afford to build really beautiful houses anymore. His firm has shrunk down to about six people and they're always scurrying around setting up deals to build banks in Iran or China.

"Maybe the thing with Helen Becker is a figment of Mom's imagination," I said. "Do you think it is?"

"Probably...Dad wouldn't like someone like that."

"He doesn't have to *like* her, he just has to go to bed with her."

"I don't know....I think he has better taste than that."

"What if he ends up marrying her?"

"He won't," Lowell said.

"Lowell, listen, how do you know? Look at Patsy Berg's father. He actually *did* marry someone and he even had two little kids with her!"

"So, who says Dad has to be exactly like Patsy Berg's father?"

"I'm just trying to show you that it does happen."

"It can happen....That doesn't mean it *always* happens."

"Mom would feel awful."

"That's for sure."

"What if she killed herself?"

"Rob! Will you cool it? You're always into these disaster scenarios. They're living apart for two months. That's all."

"I guess you're right." Lowell usually is right; that's another exasperating thing about him. "Hey, Lowell."

"Yeah?"

"Look at me one second, will you? I just want your opinion."

He looked up.

"Okay, now keep that image in mind."

"What image?"

"My face...just keep thinking about it." I turned around, pulled my hair behind my ears and then turned to face him again. "Okay, what do you think now?"

"About what?"

"My hair! Which way do you like it better? With my ears showing or not?"

Lowell gazed at me like he thought I was slightly demented, as usual. "Ears, I guess," he said finally.

I went over to look at myself in the mirror.

"You don't think they look too big?"

It's funny. I don't know if you've ever noticed this, but if you always have your ears covered and suddenly you make them show, they look huge and sort of odd just sitting there. My real problem is that I want to have hair like Vanessa's—long and straight. I even tried ironing it once the way they recommended in a magazine, but I only succeeded in burning the ends off. So now I have this wild mass and it's hard to know what to do with it.

I don't think I'm any more obsessed with my appearance than any other teenage girl. I do have good points. One is my eyes. They're green, which is an unusual color, and they tilt a little bit. My eyelashes are very thick too; that's another good point. My skin is okay, except I get freckles, like Mom. My figure is fair. I used to be really tall and gawky because I reached my present height—five feet five—at the age of eleven. Now everyone's caught up to me, more or less. In fact, several girls in my class are taller than me. I'm somewhat flat-chested, but I have a small waist and long legs so it sort of balances out. My teeth used to be crooked, but I had braces for around three years and now they're okay. Lowell says my eyebrows are really nice. I never would have thought of that because they're so thick, but he says they go with my face.

The trouble is, no one seems to be madly in love with me, except Gregory Pastner, who's a jerk. This man, Mr. Leonelli, who I used to babysit for, made a pass at me, but he was this gross, typical middle-aged man who was half bald and not at all sexy. I think my math teacher, Jerry Seavey, likes me. He always calls me "kid" and teases me about not being good in math. On Field Day he said he always liked girls with green eyes. Dad says I shouldn't worry. He says when I get to college, I won't have any problems, I'll be inundated with offers. It's nice of him to think that, but I don't think fathers are all that objective.

"Your ears are okay," Lowell said. He subsided into his book again.

I went to my room, lay down and turned on the radio. They were playing this Barry Manilow song I really like. I guess I fell asleep while I was listening, because when I woke up, it was morning. Someone had come in and pulled down the shades and covered me with a blanket.

Mom, I guess.

Four

I'M GLAD I have the teaching to concentrate on this summer. What will happen with Mom and Dad is nothing I can do anything about so it really doesn't pay to brood about it. I think Mom must feel the same way. She's so busy commuting to the city and taking her courses at Parsons that maybe she doesn't have much time to wonder if Dad really is working on his novel or is just off with Helen Becker lying under some tree in Central Park.

It's too bad about Mom's art. I think she's really good, and now it's like she considers all the years she spent on it a waste because they didn't lead anywhere. She says that when we were little, it seemed like a perfect solution. She could nip into her studio when we were napping or whatever. I remember loving to go in there when I was really small, like five or six. She always let us play with her materials, clay or paints or whatever. And I always had the feeling Mom was happy when she was in there. She'd wear her old jeans and a smock and she'd get this dreamy, intense expression.

Vanessa thinks the problem is that Mom just wasn't cut out to be a suburban housewife, but felt she had to try, partly because a lot of women of her generation felt that way, partly because she'd grown up in such an unconventional home that being conventional seemed intriguing to her, exotic almost. It seems to me you have to care more about appearances than Mom and Dad seem to in order to really fit in in the suburbs. Like, we've always lived in this quite old house where the floorboards aren't quite even. We all love it, but lots of my friends, as their parents got richer, moved to bigger houses or got swimming pools or were sent to private schools. Mom and Dad never thought of moving. They made little improvements from time to time like fixing up the attic so Vanessa could use it for a room or adding to the toolshed so we could store more of our stuff there like skis or bicycles, but we never had the kind of house anyone would want to photograph for *House Beautiful.*

I never even knew Mom was unhappy about her life till the last year or so, and maybe she wasn't. Maybe just painting was enough for her and all of a sudden it wasn't. She felt like she had to get out in the world and be recognized. I can certainly understand that. I'd never want a profession where I didn't earn any money or I was at home all by myself. For that you have to have a lot of drive and inner strength, like Vanessa.

Vanessa did get the coffee-house job; she called us from New York. She went in with Wendy, but when she came back, she was in a terrible mood. I walked in from my lesson and she was standing in the middle of the living room, yelling, "It *is* a betrayal, Mom! How can you say it's not?"

Mom and Lowell were sitting on the floor. It was one of the days Mom doesn't go into the city so she was just in jeans and a T-shirt, not her city clothes, which are either a suit or something more formal. "Can't she go to college out there?" Mom asked.

"That's not the point," Vanessa said impatiently. "It's everything! She's eighteen, Mom!"

"Who?" I asked.

"It's Wendy," Vanessa said. "She's getting *married*!"

I sat down next to Lowell. "To who? What's he like?"

"A lump," Vanessa said. "He's a total *lump*. His father runs some factory for making *dental* equipment. That's what he's going to do. He's going back to run his father's factory. He's a capitalist! And he sits there saying things like, 'Oh, Wendy'll be very happy. There're lots of crafts in Oshkosh' or whatever it's called. 'She can join the Friday Club....' He wants her to join this sick club his mother belongs to where they sit around discussing current novels!"

"Hon, simmer down a bit," Mom said. "If it's what Wendy wants, if she loves him, then maybe——"

"What if she wanted to jump off the Brooklyn Bridge?" Vanessa demanded. "Would that be great too? She just thinks that because she's had sex with him and he's good in bed or something—which is hard to believe—that's a reason to *marry* him....So what if he *is* good? She'll have to get out of bed eventually and then she'll open her eyes and there she'll be in Ohio! I mean, like, this town has fifteen hundred *people*....There's one movie in town, a drive-in, and it probably shows things like *Friday the Thirteenth*."

"Did you tell her how you feel?" Mom asked hesitantly.

"No! How could I? But I think maybe I should boycott the wedding as a form of protest."

"Will it be a big wedding?" I said. I've always wanted to be invited to a wedding. I never have been. Terry's gone to six! She has dozens of cousins who are always getting married. Her parents always buy her special outfits with shoes dyed to match. She has this one pair of lavender sandals that are gorgeous.

"The whole works," Vanessa grumbled. "And I'm supposed to be maiden of honor or whatever they call it and get all dolled up in some sickening dress slathered with lace. I'm going to have to wear a hat!"

I love hats. To me it didn't sound so terrible at all.

"Sweetie, the point is," Mom said, "Wendy will be terribly hurt if you don't take part. You've been friends for so long.... Go, just do it, and who knows what will happen. She may be very happy, despite everything."

Vanessa heaved a sigh of exasperation. "Mom, that's just what I'm worried about! That she'll be happy! If she's miserable, she can divorce him and get the hell out of there. If she's happy, she'll end up *never* going to law school, *never* doing anything she's always planned to do."

"I think she will," Mom said. "I think you underestimate Wendy."

It's funny. I personally never thought Wendy was all that great, the way Vanessa did. She always seemed to me more of Vanessa's sidekick, quiet and mousy, adoring Vanessa, but not all that bright or interesting. "What color does your dress have to be?" I asked.

"Pink," Vanessa snarled. "I hate pink! I look ill in it."

Pink happens to be one of the colors that I look best in. Terry and I took a test to see what colors we should wear most, with our eyes and hair. It said turquoise blue and kelly green for her and pink and yellow for me. I wish *I* could go to the wedding instead of Vanessa! "Are we all invited?" I asked hopefully.

Vanessa shrugged.

There was a pause. Then she said, "I'm surprised at you, Mom. I thought you'd be more understanding. I mean, *you* married at twenty and look what happened."

Vanessa is not renowned for her tact. Mom turned red and looked for a minute like she might cry. "Am I such a disaster case?" she said wryly. "So I married too young?...I still have a long life ahead of me and I intend to do great things."

"Yeah?"

"Sure," Mom said, a little unsteadily. "I have no patience for those Women's Room ladies who make a career out of whimpering. It's different with Wendy, anyway. Your generation is different."

"I just never thought I'd see the day," Vanessa said. "It's going to be a real Jewish wedding. He's going to stamp on a *glass*. They're going to hire a band——"

"You like to dance," Mom reminded her.

"Sure," Vanessa said without much enthusiasm. "I'll dance up a storm."

"Don't you want a big wedding when you get married?" I asked.

"Are you kidding?" Vanessa said. "Anyway, who says I'm getting married?"

"I didn't mean now," I said hastily. "Eventually."

"I'll elope," Vanessa said.

I hope it doesn't show that I'm horribly conventional, but I think I'd like a big wedding. Of course, I won't just marry anyone and I don't want to get married that young, like Wendy. But I think it would be nice. One of the weddings Terry was in sounded like the kind I'd like. It was in a big meadow in Connecticut and they had chamber music coming out of loudspeakers on the roof. She said everyone gathered under a big circus tent for the ceremony part and afterward they ate on the grass, drinking champagne out of paper cups, like a picnic.

Lowell had taken out his copy of *Cosmos* and was reading it. I guess weddings are not that interesting to boys, even though they have to take part in them if they want to get married. Maybe I'll be the first one in the family to get married. That's possible. Vanessa will put it off as long as possible and Lowell—well, it's hard to imagine Lowell married to anyone. He's never even had a girl friend yet, even though I know this one girl in his class likes him a lot and has been calling him for years.

Mom and Vanessa went out of the room, and I lay there, imagining getting married. If I'm part of a chamber group by then, my friends in the quartet can come and we'll have real chamber music. And Terry, of course. She can wear one of those dresses from her cousins' weddings, unless she's grown a lot or gotten much fatter. I started thinking about this photo of Mom and Dad from their wedding. It's on their bureau. Mom is wearing a really pretty white dress with a scoop neck. Dad looks very serious. He has this kind of squinty expression, as if his tie was too tight. It's really too bad Mom has gained weight. When she was young, she had a real hourglass figure—full on top, but with a tiny waist.

"Lowell?" I said.

"Yeah?" He looked up with that vague expression he gets when he's been reading.

"You know, I've been thinking.... Maybe Mom should go on a diet this summer."

"What for?"

"Well, I read this book once where the wife lost weight and bought different clothes and stuff and her husband fell in love with her all over again."

"Who says Dad's fallen out of love?"

"Why is he in the city, then?"

"Rob, come on, are you going to dredge up that thing about Helen Becker again?"

"Lowell, you heard!...I didn't make it up."

"But you're blowing it all out of proportion."

"But Mom said...she said the woods are full of hungry females."

"Both of you are just crazy. He just wants to finish his novel....Okay, so maybe she's been giving him a hard time about this job thing, but——"

I sighed. "I don't know....Look, anyway, maybe while he's away she might want to, you know, go out or something."

"Go *out*?"

"Yeah."

"With who?"

"I don't know. Men, just, you know——"

"What? Rob, you're really going bananas. She's not looking for a new husband."

"Who isn't looking for a new husband?" It was Mom. She came into the room with a bag of groceries in her arms. I guess she was unloading some stuff from the car. "Got any prospects for me?"

"Mom, did you ever think of going on the Pritikin diet? Mrs. Spinelli did and she lost ten pounds."

"Is this so you can bring me to the market and sell me for a higher price?" Mom asked.

"It's *her* idea," Lowell said. "*I* think it's dumb."

"What's the idea?" Mom said, facing me.

"It's not an *idea*, really," I said slowly, feeling uncomfortable. "I just thought if Dad was going to be away all summer, you might want to——"

"Make the local singles scene?" Mom said wryly.

"No, just——"

"I *told* you it was stupid," Lowell said.

"May I present you with some salient facts?" Mom said.

"Sure," I said.

"You see before you a forty-year-old mother, five to ten pounds overweight, lousily dressed, too many freckles——"

"I *like* your freckles," Lowell said.

Mom smiled. "Hair, once admired as a true carrot red by connoisseurs of that shade, among whom can be counted the late departed Joel Vey, now of 420 Riverside Drive."

"Late means dead," I said.

"Late means he was often late," Mom said. "Now you two might think that this same forlorn creature, abandoned after twenty years of domestic labor, unemployed, would be on the shelf, as it were—time for a tune-up and all that."

"*I* never said that," Lowell said.

"Okay, well, I just want you to know that this very morning an exceedingly presentable young man who was selling me some peaches said that I was the woman he had been looking for all his life. He was thirty! Get *that*, kids! And he thought *I* was a mere thirty-five."

"What'd you say?" I said, really fascinated.

"I told him I was otherwise engaged and went my merry way....But, I mean, doesn't this go to show? Here I am, still getting offers, right? Even with my chubby frame and graying hair."

"Mom, you look great," Lowell said.

"See, that's why we have sons," Mom said.

"Rob, have a son one day. They don't mind your freckles, they boost your ego when you're feeling down."

"Mom?" I said, still feeling uncomfortable.

"Yeah?"

"The thing is, I just said that about your figure because, you know, what you said about Dad and his maybe——"

Mom held up her hand. "Okay, let us face the facts. There is Joel, alone in the city, right? He's cleared out, no screaming wife, no noisy kids. Alone, in a wood-paneled study, the works....So, one night he's having dinner with some pleasant person, some pleasant divorced or single person, and he says, 'My wife, my life, it's all a shambles. I have such *angst*,' etc. etc. And she says, 'Oh, you poor, *poor* thing. How you must have *suffered*.' And he, looking deep into her big blue or whatever eyes, says, 'Why don't you come up and look at my etchings?'"

"Mom," Lowell said. "You're making Dad sound like a total jackass."

"In what way?" Mom said. "Because he falls like a ton of bricks for the oldest line in the world?"

"Yeah."

"Look, stronger and wiser men have fallen for even bigger piles of bullshit. The point is this: he wants commiseration, he wants sympathy. So he'll find it...And I could be five feet ten with a bust out to here,"—she indicated ample curves—"and a behind the size of a penny and it wouldn't make a damn bit of difference."

Neither of us said anything.

I swallowed. "I just thought, like, if you looked better, you might feel better and——"

"And what? And stop yelling? And be transformed into sweet-tempered, genial old Mom?"

"The way you used to be," I said, hoping she wouldn't get mad.

Mom looked mournful. "Hon, the way I used to be is over. Okay? Gone, dead, whatever. It's no use crying over it. This won't last either. We had twenty years of groveling and sexist garbage, now we'll have a few months or whatever of rage and fury, and eventually, lo: a mature and wiser Mom who will be interviewed on TV for the secret to her inner calm."

Lowell laughed. "Sounds terrific."

"It's going to be...this Mom, this future Mom is going to be so serenely mature and sensual and *wise* that men will be lining up for miles around just to engage her in a few words of conversation. Wait and see."

"But how about Dad?" I said.

"How *about* him?"

"I mean, what's going to happen? Will he come back?"

"Honey!" Mom said. "I was born with many dazzling gifts, but I'm not psychic, okay? What will be will be. He'll come back or he won't come back. He'll finish his novel or he won't finish his novel. He'll screw Helen Becker or he won't."

"Do you want him to come back? Do you still love him?" I said desperately, knowing maybe I shouldn't ask, except Mom always says we should ask anything we really want to know.

Mom's face became pensive. "I don't want him to come back now. I want to—remember that play we saw?—I want to get my act together first. I want to be a *person* again, you know, my old lively, witty, ebullient self."

"You *are*, Mom," Lowell said intensely. "You are that *now*."

Mom hugged him. "Oh, Lowell, I don't know...no, I'm not. I'm a screaming, hairy mess right now. Take it from me."

Lowell hugged her. "You're *not*...stop saying that."

Mom smiled. "Okay, not a word more....But, kids? This will be a rough summer. I mean, apart from all this, I'm taking three courses and it's a lot of work so I may not be around that much, either literally or figuratively....Will you be able to cope?"

"How can you ask?" Lowell said.

He's great at lines like that. I love Lowell.

Five

I WISH so much Terry were around this summer! She's the best person I know to talk to about personal things. I keep wondering how she'd react to what is going on in our family. Terry has always liked my family a lot, maybe because in some ways hers is a little odd. What's odd in hers is that her father is twenty-five years older than her mother. So whereas her mother is around Mom's age, forty or so, her father is in his late sixties. He's a plump, sweet, friendly man, a little hard of hearing, but he's more like a grandfather than a father. For years Terry's mother went around saying she was a rebel without a cause and she needed an outlet for her energies. I guess she was starting to find Terry's father sort of stodgy and dull. She said arguing with him was like playing tennis with yourself—she had to keep running back and forth to argue both sides because he would just sit there genially, nodding at her. Then she got a master's degree in business administration and ever since we've been in junior high, she's commuted into the city with Terry's father to work in some big advertising firm.

Mrs. Spinelli always admired Mom for being so artistic and creative and she told me once she thought Dad was "a dream" and so lively and interesting when he talked at parties. The point is, I'm starting to wonder: whose parents are happy? Anyone's? Do they just seem happy when you're little and you don't know what's going on, or is it that they really are happy to begin with, but by the time you're teenagers, they're beginning to wonder why they ever married each other? Vanessa says she feels they have their own problems and we (meaning me and Lowell) should accept that.

"I do accept it," I said. "I just don't like it."

"Nobody likes it," she said. She looked at me intently. "Does Grandma know?"

I shrugged.

Grandma is Mom's mother. She lives in the city and once a month Lowell and I go to spend the weekend with her. This weekend we're going to be with her. Dad said we should come over briefly on Sunday to see his place. Mom and Grandma don't get along that well all the time. I think Mom thinks Grandma can be bossy and overbearing; she says she doesn't know how to "handle her." That may be true. To me Grandma is always terrific, not bossy at all, just cheerful and energetic and full of ideas and things to do. Lowell likes her too.

There's one odd thing. Grandma is living with someone, and not married. I don't think they're ever going to get married, either. His name is Jacob Lowenstein. He's a shy, quiet man whose wife died of cancer about five years ago. I gather he used to be a professor of Russian literature, but he was sort of blacklisted in the Fifties and never made all that much money, even though he's written all sorts of decisive tomes on this and that, which they even use in college courses. I saw one at Grandma's house. I think he was always a poor but scholarly person. Now that he and Grandma are living together, he lives really well because Grandpa, who was a gynecologist, left Grandma a lot of money. Every summer Grandma and Jacob travel to really great-sounding places like Angkor Wat or Prague. She pays for everything. But it isn't one of those slimy things where you suspect he's with her for her money. You can tell when you see them together that he really loves Grandma. She brings a lot of spunk and color into his life.

"Then marry him!" Mom used to say. "I don't get this."

"I was married forty *years*!" Grandma would reply. "I've had enough."

"Think how much easier it would be."

"In what way? Marriage is easy? I know all about marriage, Hope. Don't tell *me*."

Maybe Mom feels differently now that she and Dad aren't getting on that well. Or maybe, now that Grandma and Jacob have been living together for four years, Mom's given up.

It's interesting how different Grandma became after Grandpa died. I don't remember Grandpa that well—I was eight when he died—but he was a self-confident, booming person who made a lot of money on the stock market. While she was married to him, Grandma was sort of quiet and shy, sometimes making these wry little cracks out of one side of her mouth. Now, maybe because of Jacob—or maybe just because—Grandma has really blossomed out. Possibly she was like that all along, but before she was somewhat in Grandpa's shadow.

After Grandpa died (just to give you an example), Grandma went with a friend of hers to look at one of those retirement villages that elderly people sometimes live in later in life. Grandma hated it at first sight, but while she was standing outside with her friend, a man who had been sunning himself by the pool rushed over. He was a widower and evidently he thought Grandma looked snappy in her red pantsuit. They got to talking, he took her phone number and that same night he asked her out. On their second date he asked her to marry him! Mom and Dad and everyone thought it was a great coup, getting a marriage proposal at Grandma's age. He was quite rich and had no defects that anyone could see. But Grandma turned him down flat. She said he was too conservative, not her type.

Grandma is not really pretty in a regular way, but I think she has what you'd call style. She has a big hawklike nose and very bright dark eyes. She dyes her hair a sort of reddish brown color. I must admit the way she dresses is slightly odd. She'll never just go into a store and buy a dress—even when Grandpa was alive, she wouldn't. What she'll do is go to some thrift shop on Third Avenue or the Salvation Army and pick up some bolt of strange fabric that was really meant to cover a chair or something. Then she'll take it to this little eighty-year-old man in the Bronx named Mr. Laskoff and have him make her a suit or dress out of it.

I once went up to Mr. Laskoff's with Grandma because she wanted to give me a Christmas present of a long red wool skirt with black Mexican embroidery. The skirt was nice, but to fit it on me, Mr. Laskoff, who was slightly deaf and maybe a little blind also, kept kneeling on the floor making me turn slowly around in a circle, patting me all over. He said he had to get the fit just right. Grandma stood right there, yelling jokes at him in Yiddish, so I couldn't say anything, but I was glad when it was over.

When Terry and I once met Grandma to see *Hair,* she came in a mink coat Grandpa had bought for her and a pair of sneakers! Terry's never gotten over that. Grandma plays tennis every day with these women friends and she told us she'd come straight from the court. She even had her tennis racket in a huge old paisley bag she likes to carry around. She always says she can't stand furs, that it makes her uncomfortable to have the pelts of dead animals slung over her back. But Grandpa wanted to get it for her and I guess she doesn't want to offend his memory by not wearing it. Also, it's warm.

When there was a bus strike in New York, Grandma used to stop and pick people up off the streets and drive them home, to Harlem or Greenwich Village or wherever they lived. I was with her once and it was a little embarrassing because she started chatting away with these people as if she'd known them all her life. That's what she's like. Mom almost had a cow and Dad said Grandma was a naive fool and could've gotten both of us killed, but Grandma said nonsense. "If I'm not old enough to take care of myself now, when will I be?" she said. I believe Grandma is sixty-five.

The day we went in to see Grandma, July tenth, Lowell and I took the Red-and-Tan bus into the city. It runs every hour and you can get it right in front of the post office. It lets you out at the George Washington Bridge and from there you can take a subway to Grandma's apartment. It really doesn't take that long, only about an hour door to door.

Grandma lives in a quite fancy building on Central Park West called The Eldorado. Her apartment has three rooms: two bedrooms and a very big living room. Grandma has one bedroom and Jacob has the other. When we sleep over, Lowell and I sleep in the living room. Jacob's room is nice. It's a bit messy and has a huge desk in one corner. In her bedroom

Grandma has a big color TV, which Lowell and I often watch since at home we just have this dinky black-and-white one.

When we arrived Grandma was standing near the door, drinking a cup of black coffee and reading *Women's Wear Daily*. She has a friend, Alma Epstein, who's in fashion and who gives her old copies of fashion magazines. Grandma was wearing a new purple pantsuit with a bright pink blouse underneath.

"Pretty jazzy," I said.

Grandma grinned. "Yeah, it kind of socks you right between the eyes, doesn't it? Okay, kids, drop your stuff. We have to get moving."

"Where to?" Lowell said, bringing our stuff into the living room.

"We're meeting Jacob at Wurlitzer at two...I'm getting him a cello bow for his birthday. He's seventy today."

"Wow!" I said. "Did he pick it out yet?"

She shook her head. "He thought you might want to help, Robby. Look, I know from beans about it. I'm just going to foot the bill, as they say."

"What a great present," I said. "That's really nice of you."

"Well, I've got to unload this cash somehow.... When the revolution comes, you don't want to be stuck with too much dough."

"You don't want to be stuck with a twenty-five thousand dollar cello bow either," Lowell said dryly.

You may not know about cello bows. The fact is, a good cello bow—the ones made in France in the nineteenth century—can cost twenty-five thousand dollars or more simply because they aren't making them that way anymore. The best ones are made by Peccatte, Tourte, and Voirin. You'd be surprised what a difference it can make, just having a first-rate bow. Of course, a first-rate cello could be even more expensive, a hundred thousand dollars or more.

Jacob is an amateur cellist. I'm not putting him down. He plays with a lot of soul. There are those who play with soul and those who play with a lot of technique. My personal preference is for those who play with soul, though of course to be really good, you have to have both. Sometimes at night, when Lowell and I are sleeping over at Grandma's, we hear Jacob playing his cello at two or three in the morning. He has his own bedroom and he always closes the door so he won't disturb anyone. He says late at night is the best time to play.

When we got to Wurlitzer, Jacob was waiting inside, rubbing his hands together. I guess he didn't want to go up without us.

"Jake, I thought you'd have it all picked out and wrapped up," Grandma said.

"Liz, you don't just pick out a twenty-thousand-dollar bow in five minutes," Jacob said. "Darling, let Robin tell you. This may take several hours."

"Of course, Granny," I said, shocked. "What did you expect?"

"Well, you two are the experts. As I said, I'm only here to foot the bill. I'll tell you what. You go up and do all the trying out or whatever and I'll do a little shopping. I'll pick you up—when? What would be good?"

Jacob considered. "Two hours? What do you say, Robin?"

"At least two," I said.

"I'm going to Doubleday," Lowell said. He likes to just stand around and read.

"Okay, well, let's all meet back here at four, then," Grandma said.

The room with the cellos was upstairs. It was a beautiful room, all carpeted and almost empty. The salesman began bringing out cellos and bows and Jacob began trying them. To start, he played the opening bars of the third Beethoven sonata. God, that was a fantastic cello! It had such a rich, creamy sound.

"Dushechka, play it for me, will you?" Jacob said. "I can't hear so well when I play it."

I felt really funny even touching the cello. It was like meeting some famous person you admire. I felt I ought to cross myself or whatever religious people do. I sat down very carefully and took up the bow. It was beautiful too. Luckily, I know the Beethoven fairly well since it's one of the pieces I had to learn for the school assembly. Wow, did it sound different! You wouldn't believe how good I sounded. All because of the cello and the bow. It was like playing on silk.

Jacob tried over a dozen bows. Of course, the cellos were all so good, it was hard to judge the bows. I played the prelude of the first Bach suite, which is one of my favorites. I hate musicians who make too big a thing about tossing their hair and looking intense but since it was just the two of us, I really threw myself into it. They used to say Jacqueline Du Pré looked like she was making love with her cello. That's how I felt. I swear, I would have married that cello on the spot; I felt really carried away. Time didn't exist. I could have stayed there eight hours, eight *days*, even. How could Jacob pick? It was like an orgy. We both played every piece we knew, practically. The salesman just stood there deferentially. Compared to some of the great players who've been in there, Jacob and I were hardly anything to faint over, but you'd never have known that from the expression on the salesman's face. I think that was one of the best afternoons of my entire life.

At four Grandma appeared; Lowell was late.

"So, what's with it, kids? What's the choice?"

"I think the Peccatte," I said. "Don't you, Jacob? I mean the second one."

Jacob opened his mouth to speak. "I think——" he began. He tried again. "I think——" Then he broke down and burst into tears. "I can't," he kept saying. "It's *too* good, it's too beautiful."

I guess I must have been quite keyed up too because seeing Jacob standing there, crying, *I* burst into tears. There we were, the two of us, leaning all over each other, blubbering like idiots while Grandma stared at us, goggle-eyed. "He's right," I kept muttering between gasps. "It's *too* good, Granny."

Grandma shook her head. "This I do not believe," she said. She turned to the salesman. "Listen, could you wrap this thing up——" she pointed to the bow we had chosen—"and take care of the bill while I make arrangements for these two to be sent to Bellevue?"

Finally we quieted down. It must have been excess of emotion of something like that. By the time Lowell showed up, we were just at the sniffing and exchanging tissues stage. Grandma was still shaking her head. "I'm not going to tell Lowell about this," she said. "He won't believe it anyway."

"What won't I believe?" Lowell said. He had the dazed, bleary-eyed look he gets when he's been reading all afternoon. "Hey, what happened? Are you okay?"

At that, for some reason, both Jacob and I began to laugh hysterically. We couldn't stop. All the way to the Russian Tea Room, where Grandma was taking us to dinner, we kept doubling over with laughter. I was afraid I might pee in my pants.

"I always knew this was a crazy family," Grandma said, "but I never knew *how* crazy."

At the Russian Tea Room I ordered blini with red caviar, which I love, and Lowell had chicken Kiev. Grandma had shashlik. We all had a little vodka and Jacob got high and began reciting Pushkin in Russian. It's such a beautiful language, even if you can't understand it. It's so soft, sort of the way eggplant tastes.

"We have to get back," Grandma said. "They're coming at eight-thirty."

"They're never on time," Lowell said.

But we took a cab anyway.

Six

FRIDAY NIGHT is poker night for Grandma. She doesn't play every Friday, just every other. She plays with a group of about six or eight friends. They don't play for very high stakes: thirty dollars is the most anyone can win in an evening. Lowell usually plays too. He's very good, as you might imagine. He has a perfect "poker face," which means he never shows if he has a good or a bad hand. I'm terrible at poker. I always get nervous and everyone knows when I'm bluffing. Also, I seem to mainly get terrible cards. So usually I just sit and kibbitz or watch TV in Grandma's bedroom if a special is on. Or I help Walter Cronkite in the kitchen.

Walter Cronkite is not really Walter Cronkite. His real name is Walter Kroner. He's the husband of Sara Kroner, who has been Grandma's housekeeper for years and years. On Friday nights Sara Kroner has to baby-sit for her grandchildren so Walter comes to help Grandma out with serving snacks and stuff. He always wears a uniform, even though Grandma told him it makes her nervous. His uniform is a bit like a tuxedo, all black, but with it he wears beautiful, very bright shirts in violet or shocking pink. Walter is black and he looks really smashing in his uniform. I guess that's why he wears it. He knows quite a lot of Yiddish. Once Grandma had a party for the Polish actress, Ida Kaminska, and Walter came out and began dancing with her and telling jokes in Yiddish. She said he should visit her in Kraków someday. Lowell and I are always planning to learn some Yiddish jokes from him, but so far we haven't. Grandma says Walter is a man of great poetical erudition and has a "marvelous gift for languages." He's also an exceptionally nice person and doesn't mind if Lowell and I sit in the kitchen and help him wrap bacon around water chestnuts. He works for Western Union during the day.

When we got back to Grandma's, Grandma went into her bedroom to change and Jacob went into his bedroom to practice with his new cello bow. I hoped he wouldn't start to cry again. Grandma changed into her patchwork skirt which was made by a lady in Kentucky. It's quite beautiful, all different patches. With it she wore her black blouse and her barometer necklace. All her jewelry is going to me when she dies, she says.

The guests that night were Alma Epstein and her husband, Isidor, and Grandma's friend from college, Lottie Mandel, and her friend, Marvin. Isidor and Grandma had a terrible fight the last time we were here. I didn't think we would see them again, but I guess they made it up because Grandma rushed over to hug them as they came in. The trouble was this: Isidor is head of the Soviet news agency, Tass, and he's extremely left-wing in terms of politics. I must say Grandma is quite left-wing herself, but about ten years ago she became friendly with some Czech journalists in New York and when the Soviets invaded Czechoslovakia in 1968, she had a complete change of heart and is almost against the Russians, which I never thought she would be. She says she still loves Russian culture, though. Anyhow, Isidor was taking this hard line about the Czechs and Grandma got almost hysterical because that morning the *New York Times* said this journalist friend of hers had been put in jail.

"I kept telling him not to go back," Grandma

kept saying. "I kept telling him...I *begged* him."

"If he went back, he has to face the music," Isidor said.

That drove Grandma up the wall. "What do you mean—face the music?"

Anyway, you can imagine the rest. The upshot was that Grandma had to be dragged off to the kitchen by Jacob and Walter, who tried to calm her down. Jacob, though he was born in Russia and looks very Russian—high cheekbones and an Asiatic, crinkly face with tufts of white hair on each side of his head—is not that interested in politics. I guess he is what you would call apolitical. He kept stroking Grandma on the arm and saying, "Don't *take* it so hard, Liz, darling." Walter kept urging her to drink the big vodka sour he had made for her. Somehow, with the vodka sour and the stroking, Grandma calmed down.

Isidor's wife, Alma, didn't interfere at all. She's a big woman who always wears brightly colored velour hats, which she keeps on all during the poker game. She chain-smokes Schimmelpenninck cigars. Since she works in the fashion industry, she wears things like checked blouses with polka-dot jackets. Grandma always says she can bring it off.

Lottie Mandel is an old school friend of Grandma's. She's quite fat and very ugly. I know it's not very nice to call someone very ugly, but in this case it's true. Unfortunately, she doesn't seem that bright either. She's the type who, if aces were wild in one game, will think they're wild in the next, even though she's been told they're not. Marvin is this man she's been dating for years. You can tell they'll never get married. I guess Grandma feels sorry for Lottie because she's so ugly and not married and not that good at poker or anything. Otherwise you wouldn't think they'd have much rapport, since Lottie isn't at all cultured or anything that great. Marvin is tall and not bad-looking. I'm not sure why he dates Lottie. I think Grandma said he's very attached to his eighty-year-old mother who still lives with him. Maybe that explains it.

There was a special on TV so I went into Grandma's bedroom as soon as the poker game began. It was called "Our Vanishing Wildlife" and since I'm fond of animals, I enjoyed it quite a lot. When it was over, I wandered out and hung over Lowell's shoulder, which he hates me to do. However, I always feel I can learn something from watching how he handles his cards.

"What're you asking me questions like that for?" Isidor was saying, showing Marvin some cards. "All I know is I have a full house, that's all."

"I'm out."

"Good, good, glad to see you go."

"Here's what you would have gotten, Marvin, my fine fellow."

"That's all I needed."

"I like a definitive game where you either get cleaned out or clean up."

A little while after that Walter brought out all these snacks and beer. I made myself a hot pastrami sandwich with some really yummy rye bread. Then, gradually, everyone went home. Lowell and I rolled out our sleeping bags and fell asleep in Grandma's living room. At about two A.M. I heard Jacob playing Massenet's Meditations. It sounded lovely. I lay awake, listening for quite a while, but finally I fell asleep.

Grandma is not a big breakfast eater. She has half a grapefruit with Brownulated sugar on top and a mug of black coffee. She says she used to be dieting and now she's just in the habit. But Jacob had gotten up early and picked up all this great stuff at Zabar's: pickled herring, fresh bagels, lox, cream cheese chopped up with chives. It was a great feast; I was starving.

While I was fixing another bagel, Lowell came back into the room. "Dad says three would be okay," he told me.

"For what?" Grandma said.

"We're going to stop off and see Dad on our way home," I explained.

Grandma looked startled. "What do you mean? Stop off where?"

I cleared my throat. "Didn't Mom tell you, Grandma? Dad's spending the summer in the city. He wants to finish his novel."

"What novel?" Grandma looked very suspicious, like the whole thing was some undercover plot.

"He started a novel about ten years ago," Lowell explained, "but he says it's hard to work at home because of all the distractions."

"Distractions?"

"You know—us, Mom, the phone ringing."

Grandma still looked suspicious. "Where's he staying?"

"At his friend Leo's," Lowell said. "He's a professor at Columbia, but he's gone to Italy till September."

Grandma looked from one of us to the other. "What does Hope think of all this?"

"All what?" Lowell said.

"The novel, taking off like that..."

"Well, she's kind of busy," I said, feeling uncomfortable.

"So things are hunky-dory with the two of them?"

I looked at Lowell. "Well, not hunky-dory, exactly."

"Come on, kids. I can take it. Spill the beans."

"See, Mom has been kind of upset this year," Lowell said, "because she wanted to get a job and she couldn't because all these people told her she didn't have enough experience or an advanced degree."

"So she felt sort of shitty," I went on, "and then she and Dad started to have all these fights. He said it wasn't his fault she was in a bad mood."

"*She* said," Lowell continued, "that they'd had a sexist marriage and that he had had a career and she'd just had us——"

"*Just* had you?" Grandma said.

"She said we were growing up, and what would she be left with?"

"So they kept on screaming," Lowell said.

"And finally he said he couldn't take it any more and he was coming to New York for the summer." I hesitated. "And *she* says he's going to have an affair with someone named Helen Becker."

"Who's she?" Grandma said.

"She works in Dad's firm," I said, "and she's really pretty."

"She's a jerk," Lowell said.

"She's blond and thin and divorced and earns thirty thousand a year," I said.

"Uh oh," said Grandma.

"What do you mean, 'uh oh'?" I asked.

"I mean, blond, thin, divorced and thirty thousand a year spells trouble.... Does she hanker after him?"

Hanker is an odd word. "I don't know," I said.

"She'd probably hanker after anyone, she's such a dope," Lowell said.

"Does *he* hanker after *her*?" Grandma wanted to know.

"No!" Lowell said.

"Lowell, how do you know?" I said.

"Because he's not that dumb," Lowell said.

"He'd have to be really dumb to fall for someone like her."

"Well, my dears, when mid-life crises strike, wisdom, which rarely plays a great role in these matters in any case, flies clear out the window."

"What do you mean?" I said nervously. "Do you mean he'll have an affair with her and marry her?"

"Marry! Who's talking about marriage?"

"Well, an affair, then."

"Why don't you ask him?"

I looked at Lowell. "Should we?"

"He wouldn't tell us the truth."

"And what about Hope?" Grandma said. "Anyone lurking in the wings for her?"

"Grandma, come *on*," Lowell said. "Mom's not the type for that kind of thing."

"She's not? How come? Does she have a terminal illness?"

"She loves Dad," I said.

Grandma sighed. "Love and marriage."

"What about them?" Lowell said.

"They were too young, is what," Grandma said.

"Mom and Dad?"

"Look, she was nineteen, he was twenty-one...They were babies!"

"But they were in love."

"Sure, but she'd gone out with one other person, that was it, I forget his name....They didn't know anything about life, about sex, about each other."

"But if they hadn't gotten married we wouldn't have been born," I told her.

"True," Grandma said. "Well, they'll probably work it out.... It can be rough, though. Poor Hope. I told her. I said—anyone who moves to the suburbs pays for it in blood. I told her that a million times."

"It's not the suburbs, Grandma," I said. "This could have happened in New York."

"Nope," Grandma said blithely. "Here she'd have a job, she'd have kept fit, given Helen whatever-her-name-is a run for her money."

"Well." Lowell and I just sat there, looking at her glumly. None of that was much help now. "I guess we should go to Dad's," he said.

At the door Grandma hugged us. "Listen, keep me posted, kids, will you? No more secrecy. I'm part of this family too."

"Sure," Lowell said.

"Grandma?" I said. "Could you not tell Mom we told you, though? I think she's going to tell you...but could you, when she does, pretend it's the first you've heard about it?"

Grandma winked. "You can count on me, sweetie."

Seven

BEFORE WE went home, Lowell and I went up to see the apartment Dad was living in. It was an old apartment house near Columbia University. There was a huge lobby with marble floors, but the elevator was dark and went really slowly. In the apartment next to Dad's someone was singing opera.

"Hi kids," Dad said, showing us in.

It wasn't much, as apartments go. I guess I'd been expecting something glamorous, like the apartments you see in the magazine section of the Sunday *Times*, with built-in bookcases made of chrome and huge paintings of one lettuce leaf. Instead the furniture was old and tweedy and there were lots of books and magazines lying around. There were only two rooms, a living room and a bedroom. The kitchen was tiny and narrow with the smallest window I ever saw.

I saw Dad's typewriter on the desk in the corner of the bedroom. "Are you getting a lot of work done?" I said.

"It's only been three weeks," he said. "There are good days and bad....Some days I really hum along, and then look at it in the morning and throw everything out."

"But is it easier working here?" I said. At home Dad's study is big and sun pours in. It's just a more cheerful room in general.

"There's something about a strange environment that's helpful," Dad said. "You don't have all your usual associations."

I knew we weren't talking about what we seemed to be talking about. But Dad is like that. He just doesn't say personal things. I cleared my throat. "Mom started her courses last week," I said.

"Oh?" Dad said. His face got a blank, impassive look.

"She had to design this clock for one of them and it's really interesting. It's like the numbers are melting off the clock. The teacher really liked it."

"Hope has a good sense of design," Dad said,

but stiffly, as though we were talking about someone not important at all.

I couldn't think of what else to say. That sounds dumb since it was my own father and usually I can talk to Dad quite easily, but everything I thought of to say seemed connected to his not being at home. "I guess it must be sort of lonely here," I said finally, looking around.

Dad shrugged. "Well, I know a few people."

"Who?" That just bounced out before I could stop it.

"Just friends from here and there...mostly, I stay by myself, but I get out a little."

"You could have dinner with Mom when she comes in for her courses," I suggested brightly.

Dad hesitated. "Yes," he said. "I could."

"I think she'd like to," I rushed on. "I think she misses you."

"Do you?" he said, in a funny, flat voice.

"I miss you, Dad," I said, looking up at him. "A lot."

"I miss *you* a lot too, Rob," he said softly.

Then come home! I thought silently. Don't have an affair, just finish your novel and come *home*. I don't know if he heard my thoughts. He just said, "Why don't you and Lowell come in the weekend after next and stay with me the whole time?"

"Sure," I said. "We'd like to....Dad, Vanessa got a job in a coffee shop in the Village."

"I know," he said.

"How?" I was surprised. I didn't know he and Mom were still talking to each other.

"She called me."

"Grandma didn't even know you were here!...I guess Mom didn't tell her yet."

He got that blank, noncommittal look again.

I felt depressed on the way home. I guess I'd been secretly hoping Dad might really be miserable, unable to work at all on his book, lonely, forlorn, missing us, ready to pack up and come back. But it's clear that's not the case at all. Dad likes New York. It's his home town. There probably are a lot of interesting things to do and maybe it is easier working without all of us around to bother him. Well, he should have thought of that when he had children! He shouldn't have *had* us if he didn't feel like spending time with us. That's not fair.

When we got home, Vanessa was trying on the dress she'd bought for Wendy's wedding. Mom was kneeling on the floor, pinning up the hem. It's a beautiful dress—deep pink with a full, full skirt and lace coming down the front. Vanessa isn't as buxom as Mom, but the dress did make her figure look really pretty. She'll look a million times prettier than Wendy, that's for sure. When she saw us, she struck a pose. "The blushing bridesmaid...what do you think?"

Lowell nodded approvingly. "Not bad."

"You look beautiful," I said sincerely.

"You've got to see it with the hat," she said, scampering off into the corner to get it. She put the hat on. It was a big straw hat with pink ribbons going down the back. "Do you think the hat is gilding the lily?"

"I'd take the ribbons off," Mom said, sitting back on her heels, surveying her.

"I like them," I said.

"I'm afraid I'm going to look like something out of *Gone With the Wind*," Vanessa said with a worried frown.

"What's wrong with that?" I said. I took the hat from her and put it on.

"You look cute, Rob," Mom said with a tired smile.

I went over to the mirror and looked. I did look nice. Why isn't anyone *I* know getting married?

"So, how was Dad?" Vanessa asked. Imagine! Asking right in front of Mom like that.

"He says he's getting a lot of work done," Lowell said.

"He seems sort of lonely," I said, not looking at Mom who was bent busily over her sewing kit.

"Loneliness is necessary for artistic endeavors," Vanessa said. "Artists *need* to be lonely."

"He wants us to come in the weekend after next," I said. I looked at Mom. "Is that okay?"

"Why shouldn't it be okay?" Mom said.

"Maybe he can come down to Giorgio's," Vanessa said. "Alice Walker is reading next week. He might like to hear her."

"*I'd* like to hear her," Mom said quickly. "I'll be in next week."

"Sure, you can come too, Mom," Vanessa said, as though she knew she'd hurt Mom's feelings. "Why don't you?"

Maybe Mom and Dad will *both* come. Maybe they'll start talking and...Maybe I better stop thinking like that. I remember how Terry and I used to hate those kids' books where the kids would have some cute plot to bring their parents back together and it would work. It doesn't work like that in real life, that much I know. There are always lots of things they don't tell you, even if they're open in general like Mom and Dad.

I followed Lowell into his room. "Lowell?"

"Yeah?"

"What do you think about what Grandma said?"

"Which part?"

"About Mom and Dad being babies when they met, being too young."

"I don't know."

"Do you think that's it?"

"Rob, what's 'it'? There is no 'it.'"

"The 'it' is that he may have an affair with—okay, so I won't say her name—with someone. Even Grandma seemed to think it wasn't all that unlikely."

"I think women make a big deal out of all this stuff."

I sighed. "I get the feeling Grandma thinks

they rushed into it.... She said once she thought they should at least have lived together a few years."

"I don't think too many people were doing that in that era," Lowell pointed out. "It was the Fifties, remember."

"I wonder how they met," I said dreamily. "I wonder if it was love at first sight."

Lowell shook his head. "It wasn't."

"How do you know?"

He looked a little embarrassed. "Well, Dad once told me about it. We had one of those classic talks about how sex isn't meaningful without love and——"

"You did? You never told me!" I felt excited. "So, go on. What did he say?"

Lowell hesitated. "I don't know if Dad wanted me to repeat it."

That got me furious. "Lowell, you are telling me right now and I mean it! They're my parents too, remember. Why should *you* know and not me? You don't even *care!*"

"Well, will you promise not to go blabbing about it to Terry Spinelli and all your little friends?"

"Lowell!" I advanced toward him menacingly.

"Okay...well, it's freshman year, right? Dad was going out with this Italian girl, Pat Graziola, but she had a boy friend back home so nothing much happened between them."

"Did she *really* have a boy friend back home or did she just say that?"

"I don't know...look, she's not going to play a major role in the story, so it doesn't really matter....The point is, Mom was also going out with a guy, I forget his name, whom Dad knew, and he used to run into them on campus a lot. Sometimes the three of them would go for coffee or whatever. But Dad figured she 'belonged' to whatever-his-name-was."

"Tom," I said.

"Tom what?"

"Just call him Tom. I want him to have a name, not just 'whatever-his-name-was.'"

Lowell smiled. "So, sophomore year begins and Dad ran into Mom, and Tom whatever-his-name-was had transferred to another school...out of the picture, totally."

"Poor thing."

"Dad said the first thing Mom said to him practically was how she'd been attracted to him from the first time they met and thought he was great and...well, I guess he felt really flattered. Anyhow, that afternoon they did it, quote unquote, and, according to Dad, it was this great, mystical experience. His conclusion was: it's worth waiting till the right person comes along because when they do—ta da!—it'll be fantastic."

I was silent a moment. "Gee, that's such a *great* story, Lowell! I *love* it! It's so romantic!"

"And then they got married and lived happily ever after."

I looked at him a little suspiciously. "Are you being sarcastic?"

"A little."

"Well, what's your point?"

"My point," Lowell said, "is maybe now he wants to sort of make up for lost time."

I shuddered. "Oh, darn! Yeah, I see what you mean."

"I mean, let's face it. Mom is great, but he's forty or something."

"Forty-two."

"And maybe he wonders what it would be like with other people."

"Like the infamous H. B.?"

"Right."

"God, I *hate* this! This is an *awful* story!"

"I thought you li͟ ͟ ' it."

"I liked the beginning. I don't like this part."

"Rob, I'm just throwi͟ ͟ up a possible explanation for a mildly possible event."

"Well, maybe he'll do it and get it out of his system and then——"

Suddenly I had an awful stomach ache. "Or maybe he'll fall madly in love! Dad wouldn't do something just for sex. He's not the type." I stood up. "This is bad....God, I *hate* this! I really do. Why couldn't they have stayed happy?"

"They tried, I guess."

"They always *seemed* happy. Remember how on Valentine's Day she used to make him those special cards? And the way they would really kiss when he came back from a trip, real kisses?"

Lowell was silent. "It'll work out," he said, not as convincingly as usual.

"You think so? Really?" I knew I was just begging for reassurance.

"Sure."

I went back to my room, but I couldn't stop thinking about it. Maybe it's better not to get married. Maybe the odds against it lasting are too great. Terry said her parents got married in a totally prosaic way. She said her mother was about to turn thirty and had had a lot of affairs with mean people who didn't want to marry her and Terry's father, whose wife had died six months earlier, proposed on the second date, and she figured: what the hell. She wanted to have kids, so she said yes.

I'm glad Mom and Dad at least started *out* in a romantic way. That's the only way I'd do it. Terry and I wrote down the kind of person we expected to marry and the kind of person we expected each other to marry. There wasn't much difference. I said I wanted someone who was sincere and smart. I don't care so much what he looks like, but I don't want him to be very hairy on his chest or arms and I'd rather he had brown eyes than blue, if every other thing about him is also good. Terry wants most of those things too, but she said she doesn't care so much if he's kind or not, she wants someone funny and entertaining. She wrote that she thought I would marry a veterinarian or chestra conductor (I think that's because I like music and animals) and that he would be sentminded, but good with children. I wrote that she would marry an actor or a very rich man who owns a big business because Terry loves clothes and only wants to work when she feels like it.

Terry showed her mother our list and she burst out laughing! What a thing to do! She said she thought we were a bunch of dreamers and you married whoever came along because you got sick of the single life. She said no man has a good sense of humor and if they're kind, they're dull and if he's an actor, he'll be unfaithful, and Terry had better have a profession because rich men run off with starlets and leave you without a cent.

I don't think she's right. I hope not! Maybe I won't find someone *exactly* like what me and Terry described, but I bet I'll find someone a little like that. I wouldn't even mind someone like Dad, only I don't want him saying mean things to me the way Dad has to Mom recently. I wouldn't mind someone like Lowell either, but Lowell is so self-sufficient. It's hard to imagine him falling madly in love with someone.

Will I find someone? Tune in again in twenty years!

Eight

CAN YOU CALL it a date when a middle-aged woman in bare feet and paint-splattered overalls has iced tea in her backyard with a man who happens to be her family lawyer? If so, Mom has been having "dates" with Ogden Haynes. He's come over a couple of times, once for dinner, once they went out to the movies. A few times they just sat around in the backyard and talked. That's where they are now. Mom doesn't seem to go all out to dress up for these occasions, but maybe it's nice for her to have someone sympathetic to talk to. I'm supposed to be bringing them lemon slices for their tea, but I'm stuck here, at the back door, listening to Ogden say, in his soft, soothing voice, "Do you still feel bitter?"

Mom gave him a dirty look. "Bitter? Who, me? Perish the thought! What's to feel bitter about?"

Ogden cleared his throat. "You mentioned that you were afraid he might——"

Mom waved her tea glass airily. "Oh look, it's open marriage, it's all the rage....Og, will you stop looking at me like that?"

"How am I looking at you?"

"With sympathy verging on pity."

"Sympathy, yes. Pity, no."

Mom sighed. "The kids want me to go on a diet, they want me to do a whole number to win him back."

Ogden Haynes patted Mom's hand. "Hope, you're beautiful. You don't have to do anything. If Joel is that——"

At this point Mom looked up and saw me, poised with the lemon slices. "Hi hon!" she said brightly. "This is really good, isn't it, Og?"

"Delicious," he said enthusiastically. "There's nothing like homemade iced tea."

Og! No wonder his wife left him. Imagine having to call someone "Og" all the time. Lest you think I am just a garden-variety eavesdropper, I should hasten to add that one reason I stopped to listen to Mom talk about Dad and our family "situation" is that there has been this truly strange silence on the topic ever since he left. Mom never mentions it. He might have sailed off to sea and not be due back for ten years. I find it sort of eerie. It must mean she finds it painful to talk about, but I wish she'd say *something*.

It's hard with Dad too. He said, "Call me anytime. I'm just over the bridge." But I just can't! If someone lives in the same house with you, you can go up and say, "Boy, I feel depressed today. I don't know why," and have one of those meandering but satisfying conversations that just spring up based on nothing. But to pick up the phone and say, "Boy, I feel depressed today——" It's harder, that's all. And whenever I do call, we chat on brightly about this and that and it all seems so hypocritical. The point is, I'm fifteen. I'm not a baby. Why can't they treat me like a grown-up instead of pretending everything is normal and fine when anyone can tell it isn't?

Vanessa is gone all the time, either to New York to work or off with her friends. I have the feeling she sees it all differently. She thinks Dad deserves "time off," as she calls it, from domestic cares, and that we should all cheer him on because it takes a lot of "courage" for someone his age to really try to do something totally different from the thing they earn a living at. I guess she doesn't take the Helen Becker thing as being that real or important.

And Lowell, who's about the only person I can

talk to, thinks my life's work is making mountains out of molehills. Deep down, I think Lowell is worried, but his way of dealing with it is to cope as efficiently as possible with everyday life. That's probably not such a bad approach. Not that I'd be capable of it in a million years.

The only other conversation that even touched on Dad's absence was when Terry's mother dropped over one Saturday. I wasn't eavesdropping this time. I was right in the kitchen with her and Mom. Mom had been describing her courses.

"So, how often do you go into the city?" Mrs. Spinelli asked.

"Three times a week," Mom said. "Yeah, it's a schlep, but I like the city...I've always missed it." Mom went to Barnard and Dad went to Columbia—that's where they met.

"I hear Joel is taking time off to finish his book," Mrs. Spinelli said. "I wish him luck. You remember that book of family chronicles I've been meaning to do? Each summer I take it out, write a grand total of ten pages and that's it."

"Well, I guess he figures this is it," Mom said. "And a friend of ours lent him his place."

"How're you coping alone, Hope?"

Mom gave her a sidelong glance. "Passably.... There are advantages and disadvantages."

"You know what I always felt about Joel?" Mrs. Spinelli said, like she was going to come out with a profound character analysis. "He works too hard. He doesn't have enough sense of play about life."

Mom looked noncommittal.

"Is he having fun?" Mrs. Spinelli pressed on. "New York can be rotten in summer."

"I think he's doing all right," Mom said dryly. "Hey, Rob, how goes it? Are you done with the towels?"

After she'd gone, Mom said, or muttered, "Dirt collecting."

I thought she meant something about the laundry. "I think it's clean," I said, looking over my pile.

Mom pointed out the door. "That one, the Pritikin diet sensation."

"Mom, I didn't mean——"

"Men have always loved my ample curves— soft, cushiony...if they want anorexics, they can go to the teenage ward at Bellevue."

In a way I know what Mom means about Mrs. Spinelli. She's almost too thin. When she smiles, it's like her skin was stretched on this very tight frame without the least bit of padding.

"Did you hear from Terry?" Mom asked.

"She wrote a postcard....It sounds like she's having fun."

Mom looked glum. I know she thinks if she was earning money, like Mrs. Spinelli, she and Dad could afford to send me on trips to Europe or fancy summer camps. Really, I don't mind about that at all. I've always enjoyed the summers right here. I like summers where you don't have a whole schedule of things to do, where you can just laze around.

"Hon?" Mom said. "Ogden was thinking of bringing his son when he comes to dinner Saturday. I thought we might all go out somewhere. Wasn't he in the orchestra with you? You could catch up on everything."

I bit my lip. "That's the weekend Lowell and I are going in to see Dad."

"You could cancel it."

I felt uncomfortable. "Well, we haven't really seen him for a while, so..."

"I thought you saw him that time you went in to see Grandma."

"Just for a few minutes."

There was a pause.

"Okay!" Mom said. "No sweat. We'll do it some other time, okay?"

"Sure," I said, both not wanting to hurt her feelings and to make it clear I did want to see Mason again. "Any other time would be great." I went off to give my lesson.

I wonder if I'm a good teacher. I give lessons several times a week now, and I keep trying to imagine what I seem like to my students. I wonder if they're disappointed at just having a teenager. The one I get the biggest kick out of is Gorman Cubberly. He's this nine-year-old who just started cello lessons this summer. But he's been taking piano for two years so he can read music quite well. I go to his house for the lessons. Can you believe this? In the living room they have a grand piano and a clavichord, and in his room, just a regular little boy's room, is an upright Steinway! It seems his father is an obstetrician, but his real love is music and he doesn't want Gorman to use the piano in the evening when he wants to practice (he takes lessons too) so he got Gorman his own piano. There it stands, black and imposing, surrounded by Fisher Price toys and a birch bunk bed.

Gorman is very formal. He always offers me something to drink and then makes an introductory remark like "I'm enjoying the Bach....It's an interesting melody." I bet he goes to a school where they wear ties and grey flannel blazers in kindergarten. If he hasn't practiced a full hour every day, he apologizes and says he'll make it up the next week. "I don't want you to feel I don't appreciate my lessons."

Talk about not having a sense of play! But I like him, he's touching and he's good too, a little stiff, but really talented. The thing with his father started me thinking about Dad, the fact that here's this man, Dr. Cubberly, delivering babies all day, but for him the high point is sitting down and playing Scarlatti on his clavichord. Maybe that's what he thinks of as he clips the umbilical cord or does whatever they do with it. So why couldn't writing be like that for Dad? Why couldn't he be an architect as a way to earn money, but have another thing that he just enjoyed? Of course, it's probably easier to play the clavichord than it is to write a novel—but then, I don't really know since I've never done either.

The night before we were due to go in to visit Dad, Lowell and I called him, just to make sure it was still okay. We got on different extensions, me in the den and Lowell in the kitchen.

"Sure, I'm expecting you," Dad said. "Mid-afternoon or thereabouts?"

"We'll be there," Lowell said.

"We can take in a movie, whatever you two feel like, really," Dad said.

"*Dressed to Kill* is playing in the Village," Lowell said.

"Ugh," I said. "I don't want to see anything gory."

"You can just close your eyes."

"No."

"We'll work it out when you arrive," Dad said, intervening. "I'm really looking forward to it."

In the morning we took the bus into the city.

"So, give my best to Dad," Mom said in an awkward way when we were leaving.

"We will," Lowell said.

On the bus I turned to him and said, "Does she still love him, do you think?"

"Sure."

"What makes you think so?"

"Well, you don't just stop loving someone overnight."

I bit my lip. "Lowell, I'm afraid Mom's going to have an affair with Ogden Haynes."

Lowell laughed. "*That's* a new one. Where did that emerge from?"

I told him about the time they had iced tea in the backyard.

"So? He said she's beautiful and he has sympathy for her."

I sighed. "Yeah, but, well, he was looking at her with this kind of mooning expression. I think he likes her."

"Why can't he like her without their having an affair?"

"Well, his wife's left him and maybe she'd, you know, want to get back at Dad if he——"

"You know what you do?" Lowell said. "You take one tiny scrap of evidence and build a whole case out of it."

I see myself standing near a huge mountain. Someone comes by and takes my photo. "Ten years ago," I say, "that was a tiny molehill. I worried it into existence." An impressive achievement, my dear....

"He's a nice guy and she likes being with him," Lowell said. "That's all."

"I wouldn't want him for a stepfather, though," I said hastily.

"Well, no one's offering him to you, so forget it."

"I'll try."

Nine

WE GOT TO Dad's around lunch time.

"Kids, listen," Dad said. "I thought I'd go down and get some stuff from the deli on the corner.... What do you say?"

"Sounds okay to me," I said.

"Sure, that'll be fine," Lowell said. He stretched out on the couch. "We're kind of beat, actually."

The air conditioning in Dad's place felt great; it was hot as a beast out. While Dad was down getting the food, I wandered aimlessly around the apartment. But there were no hidden clues, no women's slips stuffed under chairs or notes saying, "Darling, I love you. See you soon." Just as I was feeling relieved—see, nothing to worry about!—the phone rang. I answered it.

"Hello? Is Joel there?" It was a woman's voice.

"No, he's not," I said crisply. "Can I take a message?"

"Is this Robin?"

"Yeah, it is." What's it to you, lady?

"Oh well, hi! This is Helen Becker. I don't know if you remember me. I'm a friend of your parents and I...Where *is* Joel?"

No, I don't remember you at all. You're a figment of my imagination so fig your way off the phone and vanish! "He went down to get some stuff for lunch," I said. "For Lowell and me. We're staying over."

"Yes, he mentioned...Actually, maybe you could just give him a message. Joel had thought we might all get together tomorrow morning. I have a daughter about your age, Robin. I don't know if you remember her. Nina?"

"Sort of," I said as ungraciously as I could.

"Could you just tell him eleven would be fine? I made reservations at Tavern on the Green."

"Okay," I said, "I'll tell him."

"I think you'll find Nina has grown up quite a bit since you last saw her, Robin. You two ought to get along just fine....How's that talented brother of yours?"

It came back to me gradually that once years ago Nina Becker was over at our house on a Sunday afternoon and Mom and Dad got mad at Lowell and me (mostly me) for totally ignoring her and beating her in Ping-Pong about a hundred times. Was it our fault she couldn't play? She held the paddle like it was a bread pusher. "He's fine," I said.

"And you're going on with your music, Joel tells me?"

"Uh huh."

"Such a talented family!"

"Mom is getting her degree at Parsons in graphic arts," I said. "That's what she wants to do."

There was a slight pause. "I'm so glad," Helen Becker said. "Hope was always so talented in that direction. I always thought it was such a pity she never did anything about it."

I didn't say anything. Let her drown in her dumb, hypocritical remarks.

"Well! See you tomorrow!" she said brightly. "You'll tell Joel?"

No, I won't. You just go to Taven on the Green and wait for us, all dressed up with a stupid smile on your face with stupid Nina propped up next to you.... "Sure, I'll tell him."

After I hung up, I went back into the living room. Lowell had finished reading the *New York Times*. He was lying there with a bemused expression, staring into space. "Guess who that was on the phone?"

"Mom?"

"Wrong.... You have two more guesses."

"Rob, come on. Just tell me."

"The initials were H. B."

He raised his eyebrows. "What'd she want?"

"To tell us we are all supposedly meeting to-morrow for some *sickening* brunch with her *sickening* daughter....Shit! *You* said it was all my imagination," I said accusingly.

Lowell sighed. "Look, I said I just didn't think you should jump to conclusions. I still don't. Meeting for brunch doesn't mean——"

"It *does!*" I said furiously. "It does! It means they're having an affair and she called him Joel. Oh, Lowell!" I felt like crying.

Lowell patted me on the shoulder. "Rob, calm down, okay? You're just getting all upset over nothing."

"I just hate her!" I said vehemently. "She's so phony and awful! She doesn't care about my music at all! She just——" Just then the door opened. It was Dad.

He walked over and set down the paper bag containing the cold cuts. "*Voilà!*"

Lowell went into the kitchen to get some plates. While he was gone, I said, "Someone called while you were gone. Her name was Helen Becker. She said we were supposedly going to meet for lunch tomorrow."

Dad looked a little flustered. "Oh yes. You remember Helen, don't you, sweetie? She has a daughter about your age."

"Yeah, I remember....She was retarded."

"Honey!"

"She was! Look, I'm not saying it was her fault."

"Well, I saw her last week, and you're completely wrong. She's a very bright, attractive girl. In fact, I was thinking how the two of you ought to get along extremely well."

Think again! I began making myself a roast beef sandwich. "Does she still paint her nails?"

"Who?"

"Helen Becker.... She used to paint her nails these really disgusting colors like purple."

Dad was looking at me with a slightly amused expression. "Not that I recall."

"Well, I guess you'd have noticed," I said, "because it was really gross."

"I guess I would have," he said dryly.

Lowell came back with plates and napkins. He handed me one of each.

"I don't see the point of meeting her for lunch," I said, knowing I was acting obnoxious, but unable to stop. "I mean, we came in to see *you*."

"You're seeing me now."

"I just don't see the *point,* that's all."

"There's no 'point,'" Dad said a little sharply. "I thought we'd all have a good time together."

I didn't answer.

"Helen is a very interesting person," Dad went on carefully, "and I think you'll find that Nina, if you give her a chance, is too."

"Oh, I'll give her a chance," I said blithely. "But what's so interesting about her?" I could see Lowell giving me warning glances, but I ignored them.

"Helen?" Dad cleared his throat. "Well, as you may recall, she's a first-rate architect and—this ought to interest you, Rob—belongs to a leading organization for women in her field. She's supported herself and her child ever since her husband left her many years ago——"

"If she's so terrific, why did he leave her?"

Dad stared at me. "Do you not want to meet them tomorrow?"

"Not especially."

"Okay, well, then, I'll just——"

"Dad, listen," Lowell intervened. "Rob's just kind of tired....Sure, we'd like to meet them." He looked at me. "You said you always wanted to see what the Tavern on the Green was like."

I looked back at him: I did? His expression said: Cut the crap. "Sure," I said. "Why not?"

Dad looked very relieved. "Life is very difficult," he said, spreading some mustard on a slice of bread.

I looked at him, wondering if he was going to expand on that. He didn't. "Grandma says you might be going through a mid-life crisis," I said. "Are you?"

Dad smiled. "Probably. I'm at the right age."

"What does that mean?"

"Well, just, reexamining one's life, trying to decide which decisions one has made were good ones, what things can be altered and so on."

That was sort of vague. "You mean, like having a family?"

Dad looked back at me intensely. "Having a family is one thing about which I have no regrets whatsoever," he said. "You two and Vanessa are the best things I've done."

It was funny his saying it that way: the best things I've done.

"Glad to hear it," Lowell said, smiling.

"But how about with Mom?" I persisted. "Do you wish you hadn't married her or something?"

"Rob!" Lowell said.

"No, I think it's natural Robin has all these questions," Dad said. "I'm just not sure I have all the answers."

"What *about* Mom?" I persisted.

Dad paused. "Well, I think that Hope is going through a difficult time now and...that's created by certain strains which...may be alleviated eventually."

That's the way Dad talks, in a sort of roundabout way so that sometimes you don't know exactly what he's said. "Are you going to get divorced?" I blurted out.

"I don't *think* so," Dad said in a very low voice. "I don't...I don't want that to happen."

"Me neither," I said, terribly relieved to hear him say that.

"I love you both, I want our family to be together," Dad said, looking from Lowell to me. "That means a great deal to me, more than almost anything."

I stared at him. Love Mom again! I thought. Please try!

Tavern on the Green is right in the middle of Central Park. Lots of people get married there or give parties. Helen Becker and Nina were sitting at a table when we arrived on Sunday morning. Helen was wearing a bright green dress. Her hair was pulled back in a bun. She looked cool and unruffled. She still does paint her nails, but they were more pink than purple. Nina is as tall as me, but a little chubby. She has the kind of nose that people sometimes have chopped off at a certain point. Not that that's her fault either. And she has this wiry kind of brown hair that stands out like some mold growing off of her head.

"Hi, all three of you," Helen said, waving. She looked Lowell and me up and down. "Well, *look* at you two! Goodness, I'd never have recognized you.... Would *you*, Nina?"

"Yeah, I would've," Nina said.

"Isn't it a glorious morning!" she said. "I feel like you must have ordered it especially, Joel, did you?"

I looked at Dad. How can you possibly want to be with someone like that for one second? Because they're screwing, ran through my mind.

"It *is* a beautiful morning," Dad said quietly.

I wish Dad wasn't so handsome! I never did before, but now I do. He's not handsome in a vain way. He never looks in the mirror, and isn't at all conceited, but Helen Becker kept staring at him, like she was hypnotized. "I like your suit," she said finally, as we sat down. "Is it new?"

"Yes, they had a sale at Chipp's," Dad said. "You should go there, Lowell. You could pick up some good bargains."

"Sure," Lowell said. He's about as uninterested in clothes as a person can be.

"Yes, Lowell would look darling in one of those," Helen said. "He has just your coloring, Joel."

I looked at Lowell. His eyes said back: We'll discuss it later. Stay cool.

We ordered brunch. Helen ordered something called eggs Benedict and Lowell and me ordered scrambled eggs with Canadian bacon. Dad ordered an omelet and Nina ordered pancakes.

"So, how does the city strike you?" Helen said.

"Well, we come in a lot to see our grandmother," I said.

"I just love it," Helen said. "I feel sorry for anyone who doesn't live here. The cultural diversity! The people! Every day is an adventure!"

It's lucky for Helen Becker I'm not like that kid in the horror book who could turn people into flames by just thinking about it. I just sat there calmly, trying to look interested. Actually, it wasn't so much that she said stupid things as the exclamatory way she had of talking, like everything was so fantastic.

"And I hear you're working in the Rockland Library, Lowell?" Helen said. "You must get a lot of reading done.... Or is the pace too hectic for that?"

The "pace" at the Rockland Library is so hectic you could probably fall asleep for a hundred years and wake up to find that three books had been checked out. "I get quite a lot of reading done," Lowell said.

"I was so impressed by that incident Joel mentioned," Helen went on. "Where you stood up to that woman who came in to complain? That must have taken a great deal of courage."

The "incident" she was talking about took place about a week or so ago. Some lady came screaming into the library, objecting because a picture book she'd been reading to her four-year-old showed a naked child taking a bath. You'd think most people would assume that the average child doesn't bathe fully clothed, but no matter. Anyway, Lowell faced her down in his usual calm, thoughtful way and had her eating out of his hand by the time she left the library.

"There aren't too many incidents like that," he said.

"Still!" said Helen. "That's so important, staying cool in a crisis. It took me years to learn how and I still don't feel confident in those situations."

"You handle them beautifully," Dad said.

She smiled up at him. "Thanks."

They gazed at each other for a second, fondly.

Then Helen looked back at me. "And I hear Vanessa may be doing a reading at that coffee shop. That's so exciting. I'm really looking forward to it."

"It's not definite," I said. "Mainly they do published poets."

"But she'll be published *someday*," Helen said. "Her work is really remarkable, especially for a teenager."

Dad's been showing her V's poems? How awful. I glared at him.

"Nina writes poetry too," Helen said. "She's eager to hear Vanessa too."

Nina had just been sitting there quietly, picking at her food. "Yeah, I'd like to," she said quietly.

"Kids," Dad said. "Since you're finished, why don't you take a look around? We can sit here and wait for you."

Which in shorthand means they want to talk about all kinds of personal garbage which they don't want us to hear.

Nina and I followed Lowell into the park.

"You're lucky to have real jobs over the summer," Nina said. "I wish I had something to do. Everyone I know is at camp."

"It's the same where we live," I said. "I only give two lessons a week."

"I'm taking a course in ceramics," Nina said. "That's about the only good thing this summer."

"Do they let you use the wheel?" Lowell

asked. He loves ceramics and made some great pots and things for all of us at school.

"Oh, yeah!" Nina said. "It's a great place. They have all these glazes. I'm making Mom a whole set of wine glasses. I figure I can make presents for just about everyone I know by the end of the summer."

Nina isn't so bad actually. I guess she's changed. If H. B. wasn't her mother, I'd say she was fairly nice. She and Lowell got along well too. Some girls mind that Lowell is sort of small and not exactly the macho jock type, but others like him just because of that. I had the feeling Nina was the second type. Probably she doesn't have any more of a social life than me.

When we came back, I saw a sickening sight. I have terrific eyesight—it's better than 20/20—so when we were fairly far away, I could see Dad and Helen Becker, as though they were right in front of me. I felt like one of those cameras with a telephoto lens. They were still sitting at the table. But it was the way they were looking at each other! It was that kind of lovestruck, mooning look. The way Terry used to look at this total fool, Martin Darmoor, whom she had a crush on in eighth grade. Please don't let this be happening, I thought. Please let it go away.

As we came nearer, they looked up and tried to look regular. You could tell it took an effort.

"How was the park, kids?" Dad said. "Did you have a good walk?"

"Okay," I said in a subdued voice. I wanted to cry.

Later, as we walked back to Dad's apartment to get our stuff, he looked over at me with a wry smile. "So, were your direst fears realized?" he said. "Is Nina still retarded?"

Actually, my direst fears *had* been realized, but I just said, "No, she's okay."

I guess my voice sounded kind of funny because he looked at me closely. I looked back at him. It was like we both wanted to say something and couldn't. "I love you," he said finally after a minute.

I tried to smile. "Sure," I said.

"No, I mean, whatever happens, I just want you both to know that."

"We know, Dad," Lowell said.

Whatever happens! No! Don't let whatever happens happen!

"Don't work too hard," Dad said as we were getting on the bus. "Summer is for fun, remember?"

A pang went through me. What kind of fun did he mean for himself? Was Helen Becker fun? Who invented sex? If I knew, I'd call them up and yell at them as loud as I could.

Ten

VANESSA SEEMS to be reconciled to Wendy's getting married. At least she's definitely going to the wedding and so is Cooper who is Wendy's other best friend. But when Wendy isn't around, the two of them go into this sort of nasty routine which I don't think Wendy would like if she saw it. Vanessa pretends to be Wendy and sits on Cooper's lap. Wendy is really petite and Vanessa is sort of large, but Vanessa starts saying in Wendy's soft little voice, "Oh, Ramsey, I don't know what to do. Which of these toasters should we keep? They're both so lovely!" "Well," Cooper will say in an imitation deep-sounding voice. "We have to pick the one that will give my little sweetums the least trouble. Now look at this toaster. Is this the one from Great Aunt Jane? It looks just super to me. Look—it holds large juicy slices of toast." "Can toast be juicy?" Vanessa will say, looking at Cooper with big eyes. "Of course it can, my little sweet. Out here in Oshkosh we have the juiciest toast you ever laid your eyes on." "Oh, I'm so excited, Ram....But will they really accept me out here?" "How can you ask?" Cooper will say. "Of course they'll accept my little petunia, my little caterpillar."

"You're mean," I said once, watching them.

"Mean?" Cooper said. "Heaven forfend."

"Wendy's supposed to be your friend. Think how she'd feel if she heard you."

"Actually, I'm getting to kind of like old what's-his-face," Cooper said. "He has a kind of solid, redoubtable, dignified quality, if you go for that kind of thing."

"She is going to be bored senseless," Vanessa predicted confidently. "I give her six months."

"Well, six months is generous," Cooper said. "Six glorious, sex-drenched months..."

"I think what's *really* mean," Vanessa said, "is going along with it, pretending we think it's great. Is that what friends are for? To lie to you?"

"In certain circumstances, yes," Cooper said.

"So, if I'm about to marry some total jackass, you'll just say, 'Swell choice, old pal.'"

"Precisely," Cooper said. "Speaking of which, when is the great Brody due to appear?"

Vanessa's teacher, Mr. Brody, is coming to stay with us next week. Vanessa's definitely going to read at Giorgio's and she said she wants Mr. Brody to hear her. "He's done a lot of reading himself," she said.

"Can I see his poems?" Mom asked. We were having dinner. "I'd like to."

Vanessa looked uncertain. "Maybe after he's gone," she said.

"Why after?" asked Mom.

"Well, I just don't want everyone to close in around him making sensitive little remarks....I mean, he's a *published* poet, Mom."

Mom held up her hands. "Sensitive remarks! May God strike me dead. I was just intending to make dumb, prying remarks like 'Gee, Mr. Brody, you sure write a swell poem.'"

"Mom, it's not that," Vanessa said, buttering her bread. "He's just a very special person and——"

"In what way, V?" Mom asked.

Vanessa looked dreamy. "Well, he's very warm and intense, he cares about writing so much...but he's very generous too. He wants to help young poets."

"How old is he?" I asked.

"Twenty-nine."

I was really surprised. I'd imagined he was about fifty.

"Is he just your teacher?" Mom said softly. "Or is it something more?"

Vanessa turned red. "What do you mean?"

"Well, you talk about him as though you care for him a lot and I just wondered——"

Vanessa stared at her for a long moment. "We're lovers!" she blurted out. "Do you want to make something out of it?"

Mom laughed nervously. "Hon! I don't want to make anything out of it at all. I just wanted to know what kind of a visit this was, what we were letting ourselves in for."

"You're letting yourself in for meeting a wonderful, brilliant, terrific person!" Vanessa exploded. "Is that going to be such a difficult thing? Should I ask him to go to a hotel?"

"V, we're delighted to have him....I'd just like to know a little more about him, that's all."

"He's married," Vanessa said quietly, "but he's been separated for two years."

"Does he have any children?"

"He has a boy who lives with his wife." She looked at Lowell and me. "Anything you two want to know?"

"Is he a really good poet?" Lowell asked.

"Yes," Vanessa said. "Really good." She looked at me. "So, what do *you* want to know, Rob?"

"Are you going to marry him?" Maybe then V could use that same dress she's wearing to Wendy's wedding.

"What kind of family is this?" Vanessa asked, heaving an exasperated sigh. "Can't anyone be in love without rushing to get married? Steve's just getting divorced after seven years of a terrible marriage. He doesn't want to rush pellmell right into another one.... And I don't either! And if I hear one *word* from anyone in this room about marriage or anything like that while he's here, I'm never speaking to *any* of you again!"

Mom clapped her hand over her mouth. "My lips are sealed forever more."

Vanessa left the room, looking stormy.

Gee, how exciting! I wonder if Vanessa is really in love with Mr. Brody. She's been in love before a few times. Once was in her junior year of high school. It was with this foreign exchange student named Hans whose father worked for the United Nations. They lived right down the road from us. He was this very nice, friendly blond boy who always shook hands with Dad and called him "Sir." He and Vanessa used to see each other a lot. The day he left, she cried and cried. They still write to each other—I've seen the letters.

Vanessa was in the bathroom later, wrapping her hair up in a towel. I felt like asking her about Mr. Brody, but I didn't want to seem prying. Finally I said, "Do you like him as much as you liked Hans?"

I thought Vanessa might get furious at my asking, but she just said, "Oh, Hans was just a...a kid thing, Rob. Steve's a real person, a real grown-up. I'm not saying I'm going to marry him, but he's someone I can imagine living with and being with.... We might live together next year, we're not sure."

"Do you feel jealous that he was married before?" I asked. I would. I want to marry someone who's never been married or even engaged.

"Not really. His marriage is about the same as if I'd married Hans. He married a girl he'd known since junior high, a sweet girl, but..."

I sat down on the closed toilet seat, watching Vanessa brush her hair. "I guess Mom is afraid you'll do what she did, marry too young."

Vanessa threw up her hands. "But I'm a totally different person! I'm not the least bit like Mom.... She was totally into pleasing Grandma and doing what was expected of her. I'm not like that. I just want to do what will please *me*."

"But maybe it was also just she and Dad fell in love and——"

Vanessa looked at me. "Everyone falls in love."

"Sure." I was silent a moment. Then I told her about our lunch with Helen Becker. "I think maybe they are in love," I started to say. "I think maybe——"

"So?"

"But what if he married her, V?"

"He won't marry her," Vanessa said vehemently. "Not a chance in the world."

"Really?"

"It's a fling. They had a yen for each other, or something."

"But don't people sometimes have yens for each other that lead to marriage?"

"Dad's not the type," Vanessa turned to me. "I mean, let's face it, Mom hasn't exactly been the easiest person to live with the last couple of years."

"Do you think she's easier now?" Vanessa hasn't even been home this past year. She doesn't even *know* what it's been like.

"Well, at least she's finally doing something instead of sitting around screaming at everyone....But it's sad, really. She's wasted her life and now——"

"Do you think so?" I said, taken aback. "Why?"

"Because she was good! She could have really done things with her art."

"But maybe now——"

"Sure, maybe."

"Does Mr. Brody know about Mom and Dad? I mean, that Dad won't be here?"

"Oh, sure....His parents divorced when he was seven. And he's separated himself, remember."

I smiled at her. "I can't wait to meet him."

Vanessa smiled back. "I think I'll give a party while he's here, sort of half for Wendy and Ramsey and half for Steve."

"Can Lowell and me come?"

"Sure." Vanessa was curling her eyelashes. They're long already, but she presses them up and holds them in place so when she lets go, they fan out all around her eyes.

"V, are Mr. Brody and Hans the only people you've ever had sex with?"

"Steve!"

"Steve, I mean.... Was there anyone else?"

Vanessa smiled. "Oh, a couple, but no one I cared that much about.... Cooper and I did it once, but it was more——"

"I thought he was gay."

"I guess he is basically, but we always liked each other. And one night, I forget why..."

I can't imagine Vanessa doing it with Cooper! It's not just that he's quite funny looking, but he doesn't seem the romantic type to me at all.

I started thinking about Mr. Brody all day while I was giving my lessons and afterward when Lowell and I played tennis. I thought about sex in general. I've read so many books about it, but it doesn't seem to have had that much effect, as far as anything happening. The first one I read was *Forever* when I was in junior high. I really liked it. I kept wishing I could meet someone like Michael. I mean, you could tell he really liked Katherine, the way he bought her that locket and everything; it wasn't just sex. Then I read *Portnoy's Complaint* which was funny and *Fear of Flying,* but that was more about someone who's been married a long time. I wish more people would write books about teenagers who are doing it for the first time. All those other books about people who are doing it for the millionth time so they're all sort of blasé, like the regular ways are dull. I think the regular ways sound really interesting, scary, sort of, but definitely interesting.

The trouble is, reading about things doesn't seem to bring you any closer to doing them. Maybe the opposite. It's almost sort of intimidating. Terry hardly ever reads at all, and she's done a million more things than me with boys. Not "it" but all sorts of things. She once even took all her clothes off with a boy! I promised never to tell anyone this, but they really started doing it and then, in the middle, Terry said she wanted to stop. She suddenly decided she wasn't "ready." I don't know if that means she's still a virgin or not. She doesn't either. I wonder if you can be half a virgin. But she said she's glad she did it half-way because it wasn't as bad as she expected. I know people always say how great it is, but it doesn't always sound that great. She did say she liked everything that came before better, all the kissing and stuff. I think I'd like that too. I hope I meet someone who wants to do that for a long time before "it." I think I'd like to kind of work up to "it" really slowly.

Lowell and I walked home after tennis.

"Don't you think it's exciting," I said, "about V reading her stuff at Giorgio's?"

"Yeah, I bet she'll be good," Lowell said.

"Maybe some famous publisher will be in the audience and 'discover' her."

"I don't think it works that way with authors," Lowell said. "That's more with actresses."

"Dad's coming....I spoke to him last night."

Lowell just nodded.

"Do you think he'll bring *her,* quote unquote?"

"I guess."

I know Lowell hates me to talk about it, but I couldn't resist. "Lowell, do you think Dad's in love with her?"

He shrugged. "How should I know?"

"What do you think," I persisted, "just based on seeing them together that time."

"I didn't notice anything much," Lowell said. "I think he probably just likes her as a friend, someone to talk to."

I wanted so much to believe that, I almost did. "No sex?" I asked anxiously.

"Maybe they go out on dates and he kissed her goodnight or something," Lowell said, "but that's all."

"I don't think it works like that with grown-ups," I said.

"Like what?"

"I don't think they just stop at kissing."

"They do if they don't feel like doing anything else."

I sighed. "Oh, Lowell, I don't know....I'm just scared she wants a husband and she's going to pounce on him on a dark night and drag him off to her lair."

Lowell got a wry expression. "And devour him bones and all?"

"Right."

He smiled. "I don't think so."

"But remember how he said to us, 'Whatever happens, I love you'?"

"So?"

"What does 'Whatever happens' mean?"

"That he's not sure of what's going to happen."

"You don't think it implied he was planning to marry her?"

"Rob! Those two words?"

I laughed. "You think I'm jumping the gun?"

"For a change."

"Do you think she's pretty?"

"Fair."

"She has a great figure," I said mournfully.

Lowell wrinkled his nose. "What's so great about it?"

"I mean thin."

"Why is thin so great?"

"Mom used to be thin...or thinner."

"Mom is fine," Lowell said.

"She's not glamorous," I sighed.

"Dad doesn't go for all that crap."

"You don't think so?"

"Definitely not....She probably dyes her hair. It looked kind of false to me."

"They say men prefer blondes."

"Rob! Do you believe *every* dopey thing you read?"

"Lowell, listen, just tell me one thing. You definitely didn't think they were looking at each other in any special way, any lovey-dovey way?"

Lowell shook his head.

I kissed him. "Oh, I hope you're right."

"I'm always right," he said modestly.

When we got back from tennis, we went into the kitchen for some juice. Vanessa was sitting at the table with someone. He was tall with frizzy dark hair, a beard and rimless glasses.

"Steve, this is Robin and Lowell," Vanessa said.

"Hi," Mr. Brody said. "Who won?" He had a friendly smile.

"We each won one," Lowell said.

"He has a better serve," I explained, "but I'm steadier."

"When does Mom come back today?" Vanessa asked.

"Not till nine."

"Well, Steve and I are going into the city. Tell her we'll see her later."

It wasn't until the next night that all of us had dinner together.

"It's nice that you can be here for V's reading," Mom said to Steve. Vanessa said we should call him Steve.

"She'll be terrific," he said. "It's important with poetry, being able to read your own things. I'm not good at it, unfortunately. It's like acting, really. You have to be unselfconscious."

"To me writing is the intimidating part,"

Mom said, "but then that's never been my strong point...." She began mixing the salad. "Is this your first time in New York, Steve?"

"My agent's here," Steve said, "so I come in to see him every now and then."

"I didn't know poets had agents."

"Well, I'm working on a novel."

"Oh." Mom hesitated. "My husband is too. Did Vanessa mention that? That's why he's not around this summer. A friend of ours gave him an apartment and he thought it would be a good time to—well, get away. I suppose it's hard concentrating with your family rushing in and out."

"It was hard for me," Steve said.

"Is your—how old is your child?"

"He's six now."

"And you see him pretty often? That must be hard, when they're so young."

"I see him mostly on vacations. It's not often enough."

Mom poured him some more wine. "I guess families just tend to...disintegrate these days. It's a pity."

"I suppose some——" Steve started to say.

"It's good," Mom ran on. She was flushed. "There probably are too many families. I mean, why should there be so many? But it's just when you've put so much of your time and energy into it, then to see it—just dissolve—is kind of hard."

Vanessa was staring at Mom, obviously wanting her to shut up.

"I can imagine it must be," Steve said.

"Our generation just rushed into it, pell-mell," Mom said, pouring herself more wine. "Kids, marriage. We didn't stop to think."

"I don't know if that always helps," Steve said.

"Of course it helps," Vanessa said. "What do you mean?"

"I just mean, you're always taking a chance," he said. "No one's going to guarantee the outcome."

"I think the problem is men," Mom said. "They don't know what they want. They want all the traditional things—home, family, kids and they want all the fun, exciting things—younger women, adventure."

"Mom, that's such a stereotype," Vanessa said. "There are as many different kinds of men as women."

"Maybe younger men are different," Mom said pensively, ignoring her. "So I've heard."

"You're just bitter because of Dad," Vanessa siad. "Don't generalize to the whole world."

"I'm *not* bitter!" Mom snapped. "I'm trying to be a realist, for once in my life, damn it! *I'm* the one who's here, in case you hadn't noticed. I'm not the one cooling my heels in an apartment in the city waiting for inspiration to strike."

"So? Dad's entitled to time off if he wants," Vanessa said.

"Of course he is. Who's denying him?"

"Mr. Brody, Steve, did you start publishing poems when you were little?" I asked. I was afraid he would think we were a strange family, with Mom and V yelling at each other like that.

"I was in college," Steve said. "Nineteen, actually."

"I wrote a poem once," Lowell said. "It's about the Brooklyn Bridge. Our teacher told us to write a poem about the most beautiful thing we ever saw."

"Bridges *are* beautiful," Steve said, smiling.

"I'm going to build them when I grow up."

"I don't know *what* I'm going to do," I said. I reached for another roll.

"I'm going to grow down," Mom said. "Has that ever been done? Reverse the usual process.... So listen, Steve, what's your novel about?"

"Mom, he doesn't want to talk about it," Vanessa said.

"I don't mind talking about it," Steve said.

"She's afraid I'll disgrace the family," Mom said. "Look, I'll admit it, I don't read a lot of modern fiction.... But I'm interested in the process."

"It's about my twin sister, actually," Steve said quietly.

"I didn't know you were a twin," Vanessa said.

"Yeah," he said. He was silent a moment. "She died when we were both sixteen, and I guess...Well, maybe writing it is a way of bringing her back or trying to understand her life, something. Since I had Peter, it's made me see everything about childhood differently. It's like going through it a second time, but from a different angle."

"Yeah, I think that's true," Mom said. "I like that."

"For me having a kid was important," he went on. "I didn't think it would be. I wasn't prepared."

"It was important for me, too," Mom said. "I didn't mean to give you the wrong idea before, about families. I think they're the best thing. I couldn't not be part of a family. I've never—regretted that. It's——"

Just then the doorbell rang. It was Ogden Haynes. Evidently he and Mom were going to the movies.

After they'd left, we sat around a little while longer.

"Listen," Vanessa said. "She's not always like this. It was really——"

"I liked her," Steve said. "She's very direct, very open."

"I mean, you can see why Dad couldn't get anything done. She's not the most support-ive——"

"I didn't get that feeling. She just seems—scared."

Vanessa looked down. "Yeah, she is."

"She's going to be an artist," I said.

"She *is* an artist," Lowell said. "Right now."

— 134 —

"She never reads," Vanessa said. "It's not just novels. She never reads, period."

"Stop criticizing Mom all the time," Lowell said suddenly. "She does her job."

We all looked at him. It's unusual for Lowell to speak out like that.

"My mother had a hard time when my father left," Steve said. "She hadn't worked since before we were born. It's not that easy."

"I didn't say it was," Vanessa said. "But let her just do it, get on with it."

"She is," Lowell said. "That's what she's doing right now."

"Yeah," I said, glad Lowell had come to Mom's defense. "Anyway, she made lots of beautiful pictures when we were little. She just never got a gallery to show them."

"But she did them," Lowell said. "That's the point...And she had us, she raised a family."

"Big deal," Vanessa said. "What's raising a family?"

"What do you mean what's raising a family?" Lowell said. "Do you wish we hadn't even been born?"

"That's not what I mean at all," Vanessa said. "She could have had us and ten more....But she could've also gotten a job and by now she'd be somebody, not just another dissatisfied housewife ranting on about lost opportunities."

"That's a little cruel, V," Steve said gently.

Vanessa looked at all of us, sensing she was outnumbered. She sighed. "Hey, let's take a walk, okay?" she said to Steve. "I feel like getting out."

"Sure." They left, holding hands.

Mr. Brody, Steve, must be in love with Vanessa. He said, "That's a little cruel" but five seconds later he went off, holding her hand. That's because if sex is good between people, they put up with things they might not otherwise. That's what Terry says. But I felt bad. I kept thinking how if Steve had come any other summer, when Dad was here, it would have been completely different. There wouldn't have been yelling and Mom getting upset and everyone taking sides. It's not that our family was perfect, by any means, before this thing started with Mom. But at least it was sort of a unit, all of us doing things together and stuff. Now it's everyone all splintered off. It's not a good way to be.

Eleven

IT'S AUGUST NOW. This week Vanessa is giving the party to introduce Steve to all her friends. It's also a kind of prewedding party for Wendy who's getting married in three weeks. The week after this Vanessa is giving her reading at Giorgio's and after that Terry will be home from Europe. In short, the summer is ending. If it were any other summer, I'd be enjoying this time most of all. The really hot weather is over mostly, and you can start looking forward to school starting again. Once it starts, it's the same old thing, but right now you can start imagining what new teachers you'll have or what new kids might be in your class.

But this summer the fact that it's August makes me nervous. What is Dad thinking about? Is he thinking about coming home or is he thinking about staying in New York for good? We talk on the phone, and I guess I'll see him next week at Vanessa's reading, but we never talk about that.

Mom doesn't talk about him either. Partly, she really is very busy with her courses. Her teacher liked the clock she designed. He asked if he could keep it to exhibit it and maybe use it for the school catalog where they have photos of outstanding student design. Lowell and I made a big sign saying "Bravo Mom!" and hung it in the hall where she could see it when she came home.

For the party Vanessa said I could borrow one of her blouses. It's an Indian peasant blouse with embroidery going down the front. I think it's really pretty. I'm excited because Mom said Ogden would bring Mason to the party. Not that I imagine he's been pining away for me since he left our school, but he did seem to be staring at me the time we saw them in the restaurant and Mom keeps saying how he asks after me when she's over there.

Cooper brought over a lot of his records to add to Vanessa's. They fixed up the living room so there'd be enough room for everyone. There was some dancing, but mostly people sat around and talked, to the extent you could with the music going. Mason didn't come till late, around midnight. In the beginning, I mostly talked to Wendy and her fiancé. I don't think he's so bad. His name is Ramsey, but Cooper and Vanessa call him "The Ram." He's very tall with curly hair.

"It sounds like it's going to be a nice wedding," I said hesitantly. "Vanessa's dress is really pretty."

"You should see Wendy in hers," Ramsey said proudly.

"Mom's letting me wear this dress she wore when she got married," Wendy said. "It's almost a hundred years old, with real lace all down the front."

"I like old-fashioned things too," I admitted.

"Things that have stood the test of time are best," Ramsey said. He has this very deep voice. When he says things like that, they do come out sounding a bit pontifical. Maybe that's what Vanessa and Cooper don't like in him so much. But he and Wendy really seem to be in love. Wendy looks different to me, not so mousy and small, more beaming and happy.

At midnight Cooper brought in this thing he'd invented which he calls "A Light Show." He made the room completely dark and put his creation on top of the piano. It consisted of sixteen empty cat-food cans, lids off at both ends. In each one there was a colored light bulb. In the dark the lights flashed on and off in a kind of pattern. The complicated part was when he hooked it up to the radio. When the music played, the colored lights responded to the music. Also, to make it even more complicated, there was a set of dials he passed around. As you fiddled with the dials, certain colors became brighter or dimmer. It was really quite beautiful. I think Cooper wants to do something connected to electronics when he grows up.

We all sat on the floor. Cooper lit up a water pipe with pot in it and we passed it around. Vanessa and Steve were leaning back against the couch, their arms around each other. She had her hair loose and looked beautiful in a long, dark-red cotton dress that came to the floor.

I've only smoked pot a little. What I don't like is the burning sensation as the smoke goes down. But Cooper said the light show could only be appreciated if you were somewhat stoned so I thought I'd at least try.

Mason had come in when the light show was being set up. He was sitting about six feet away, just staring at me. I thought at least he'd come over and talk or something. I passed the water pipe to Lowell, who was sitting right next to me.

Mom was sitting in the corner, cross-legged. She was wearing a yellow, purple, orange and pink striped poncho and her Adidas sneakers.

"Now, what am I supposed to feel?" she said intensely, taking a big puff.

"Mom, you're just supposed to relax," Vanessa said languidly, running her fingers through Steve's hair. "There's nothing you're *supposed* to feel."

"No, but I mean, how do I know if I'm getting it?"

The pipe went around a couple of times along with the set of dials for the light show. I couldn't really figure out how to work the dials, but the lights were beautiful. Round spots of violet, red, purple throbbed in the dark, like soap bubbles, floating in space.

Suddenly Lowell began to laugh in this manic, private sort of way.

"What's so funny?" I asked, puzzled.

"Those blue lights...the way they're moving."

What's so funny about blue lights? I wondered if he was getting stoned.

"I think maybe I'm *beginning* to feel something," Mom said. "Like that pattern over the door looks very sharp and clear...is that——"

"Mom, whatever you feel," Vanessa said. Her voice sounded very slow and drifting, like she was half asleep or far away. "Just try and relax."

"I *am* relaxed!" Mom barked.

Wendy whispered to me, "I just feel sleepy."

"Me too." I looked over at Mason. He was still

staring at me. Suddenly that struck me as funny. I started to laugh.

"What?" Lowell asked, turning to me. He'd taken off his glasses. His eyes looked blurry and dreamy.

"I can't explain."

I decided to stare back at Mason. If he could stare at me, I could stare at him. It turned into a kind of game. We'd both stare as hard as we could, as though we were trying to hypnotize each other. Once he smiled and looked away and then looked back again.

"So, is everyone starving?" Cooper asked.

"Sure," Lowell said. I thought he'd fallen asleep. He was lying with his head on a pillow. "Do you need any help?"

Cooper darted off into the kitchen. I kept looking at Mason. Out of the corner of my eye I could see the colored spots of light blinking on and off. They looked almost alive.

Suddenly Cooper rushed back again and handed everyone a bowl and spoon. He said, "All right. Now folks, pay attention. This is going to be the greatest thing you've ever eaten."

What it was was Häagen Dazs coffee ice cream with hot fudge sauce poured over it. There were fresh chocolate chip cookies warm from the oven. It did taste fantastic. Maybe from eating in the dark or maybe from being stoned. I swirled the ice cream around on my tongue, trying to make it last.

When I stood up to bring my bowl back to the kitchen, Mason walked over to me. "So," he said, smiling, "who won?"

"I don't know....I feel funny. I think I'm a little stoned."

"Me too....That light show was great, wasn't it?"

"Yeah."

We stood there, looking at each other.

"Let's go for a walk," he said.

"Okay."

Outside it was an incredible August night, all insects chirping and frogs grunting and a hazy smell of wild flowers and grass. I took my sandals off.

"You've gotten taller," he said, looking down at me.

"A little."

Mason isn't as tall as his father, but he has that same solid, chunky look. His eyes are nice, brown. They have a friendly expression, like a dog that you'd want to scratch behind the ears.

We started walking slowly across the field near our house.

"This is my favorite month," I said. "August. Only this year it hasn't been that great."

"How come?"

"My parents—they've split up." I thought his father would have told him that.

"Yeah, I know. Isn't it just for the summer, though?"

"I don't know!" I wanted to ask him how it

had been for him before his mother moved out. "I think my father might have a girl friend, this woman he knows in the city. Lowell thinks I'm exaggerating it, but when we went in to see him, she was there."

"My father thinks your mother is still in love with your father."

"Is that what he said?" I said hopefully.

"Something like that."

"Are yours?"

He shrugged. "I don't know....Mom hasn't been at home for two years so I guess she's not exactly desperate to be with us."

"Do you miss her?"

"Kind of....I'm used to it now....I think my father still misses her." He paused a moment. "She's really beautiful. She used to be an artist's model when she was in college."

"You mean, like posing naked?"

Mason nodded. "We have this painting some artist did of her, lying on a dark green cloth."

I would think that would be embarrassing, knowing your mother did that.

"Sometimes, when she was away, I used to come into the den and Dad would be just sitting there, staring at that painting," Mason said. "Once I came in and he was crying. He didn't want me to see, but I did."

I was silent. "I guess it's hard for people to stay in love a long time," I said.

"Yeah, I guess....Mine were fighting so much I was kind of glad when she moved out.

At least it was quieter.... Was it like that with yours?"

I nodded. "This year.... Not so much before that. They'd fight sometimes, but.... Once, it was funny. I remember we were sitting around in the evening and Mom was reading this magazine, *The Ladies' Home Journal*? They had this article called 'Can This Marriage Be Saved?' It kind of presents two points of view, the husband and the wife, and then this marriage counselor or whatever tells what they should do to make things good again. Anyhow, Mom suddenly looked up and said, 'I'm reading this thing called "Can This Marriage Be Saved?"' and Dad, who was sitting next to her, said, 'Oh, is that the one where she tried to commit suicide?' and Mom said very seriously, 'No, she did, she *did* commit suicide' and Dad said with a kind of laugh, 'That must have been a hard marriage to save.' And Mom burst into tears and ran out of the room."

I never mentioned that to anyone before. It happened when Lowell wasn't in the room. Also, I've never been sure what it meant. Probably if Dad hadn't moved out a week later, I wouldn't have remembered it at all.

After a minute Mason said, "Your mother sounds like a very emotional person." But he didn't say it in a condemning or mean way.

"Yeah, she is," I agreed. "So's my father, though.... Sometimes I think that's the trouble.

I mean, most of the time they're okay, but when they both hit a down mood, wow!"

"I guess marriage is better when people have balancing traits, like one being calm and the other not."

"I guess so. I really wouldn't know from personal experience."

He laughed. "Me neither. I've only been married two or three times."

Then he reached out and took my hand. Usually it's awful when boys suddenly grab you and it's not at all personal, just part of some preconceived plan they've had all along. But Mason did it in a nice way; his hand felt warm and good.

When we got to our house, we sat down outside. Dad built this seat which goes around the big oak tree.

"Maybe you could come up and visit me sometime at Deerfield."

"Sure, I'd like to."

Then, before I could even get worried about whether or not he was going to do it, he leaned over and kissed me. His lips were so soft! After the kiss, we just sat there, staring at each other.

"You have really beautiful eyes," he said intensely.

"Thank you."

Then suddenly we started kissing again. Only this time it was lots of kisses all running together. Our mouths opened and our tongues touched. I always thought that would be awful, someone putting their tongue in your mouth, but it wasn't, it was really nice.

Mason put his hand up and touched my hair. I'd washed it that afternoon with a special apple shampoo I got at the Co-op. He brought his hand around my shoulder and slowly down my back to my behind. He held it there, hesitantly, as though he didn't know what to do next. I didn't know what *I* should do either. But I decided to do what I felt like doing. I put my arms around his neck. We were so close, I could hear his heart thumping. Maybe he could hear mine too. We were both sort of out of breath.

"I guess you should go in," he said breathlessly, like he didn't want me to.

"I guess." I didn't want to, but I was a little scared of what might happen next if I didn't. I used to read in books about people getting "carried away," but I never knew what that meant before.

"I'll call you tomorrow," he said softly.

"Okay." I smiled at him and went into the house. I felt like I was really walking on air. Talk about changes of mood! I must be going crazy! I mean, here I hardly even *know* him! And I really felt like I would have gone off and practically married him that minute if he'd asked me. I really must be crazy. I hope *so* much that he doesn't have a regular steady girl friend back at school.

When I was in bed, I lay there imagining

Mason inviting me up to Deerfield. I imagined us in his room and his saying he'd never done much with anyone before, but he liked me so much he wanted to. Then I imagined our kissing without any clothes on. I imagined he had a bed with a soft blue corduroy cover on it. If I knew someone was going to kiss me when I didn't have any clothes on, maybe I'd put perfume on in special places, like on my breasts. Terry said it was a nice feeling when that boy she half did it with kissed her breasts. The one thing that was awkward, she said, was when he took her hand and put it on his penis. She didn't know what to *do*! It turned out he wanted her to sort of stroke it; I guess that was a good feeling for him, so she did. I think I'd definitely feel awkward doing that, though I must admit I'd also be curious. I wonder how it feels. I mean, if it made someone feel good and you liked that person, you'd want to do it, I guess.

I'm glad Mason kissed me. At least it shows he thinks I'm attractive. I would just hate it if he had just thought I was a nice person or smart or something. Everyone thinks that about me, practically. I want to be a sex object!

Twelve

VANESSA PRACTICES every morning for her poetry reading. She and Steve go into the den and he listens to her read. I guess he gives her suggestions on how she should sound since he's done it before. She won't let any of the rest of us listen to her.

"Which ones are you going to read?" I asked.

"You'll see," she said, smiling mysteriously. Then she added, "There's one about you, Rob."

"Really?" I never knew Vanessa had written a poem about me.

"Why can't we listen?" Lowell said. "We might give you good suggestions."

"It's too embarrassing, even having your own family in the audience. I'd rather face a thousand strangers, than all of you."

Vanessa must be really nervous about this. I didn't expect she would be. I wonder if she feels nervous that Steve will be in the audience too. He's been here almost a week now, and I've gotten used to it. He sleeps in Vanessa's room, I guess in the same bed with her since she doesn't have a pull-out bed anymore. I suppose they must make love a lot. But you couldn't tell it. They do get up late, but Vanessa always sleeps late on vacations. They do seem to touch each other a lot and give each other these special glances when other people are around.

"He's a good guy," was Mom's pronouncement one day when Vanessa wasn't around.

"What do you mean?" I asked.

"I think he's mature, thoughtful."

"Will they get married?" It would be so great if Vanessa had a wedding just like Wendy's in a long old-fashioned dress. I could be a bridesmaid and wear the same dress Vanessa is wearing to Wendy's wedding.

"I doubt it.... V's got a lot of growing up to do before she'll be ready for marriage," Mom said.

"Did you save your dress, Mom? The one you were married in? Wendy's wearing her grandmother's dress."

Mom frowned. "I think so....But V would never wear that in a million years. It's too ruffly and gooey for her. I think she'll get married in a vinyl jumpsuit or something."

"Can I wear it?"

Mom smiled. "Sure, hon, if you want....You're not planning anything precipitous, I trust?"

I blushed. "No....But they say younger sisters get married first."

"True....How'd it go with Mason the other night? You were gone a long time."

I didn't know anyone had noticed. "Yeah.... Well, I think he likes me."

"I know."

"Did his father say he did?"

"He kind of indicated that....You liked him?"

I nodded. "I guess it would be funny if I married him, though, wouldn't it? Since you're such good friends with his father."

"Hon, take it slowly, okay? You're fifteen."

"Mom, I know! I'm not really going to *marry* him! I don't think I'm going to marry till I'm thirty, actually."

"Why thirty?"

"Well, I want to do lots of things. I don't want to be stuck with a baby and all that."

"Babies aren't so terrible."

I sighed. "Maybe....It's a lot of work, though."

"True."

I told Mom how Vanessa had said one of her poems was going to be about me. "I can't wait to hear it."

"I just don't know what to do," Mom said, frowning, "about the reading and all."

"What do you mean?"

"Is Joel going?"

"I think so."

Mom made a face. "And he'll probably bring Helen. I just don't know if I can sit through that."

"He might not bring her."

"Could you find out, hon? Because I think it would just be too awkward if he did."

"How should I find out?"

"Just call him and kind of insinuate it into the conversation."

I'd been meaning to call Dad anyway since we were all planning to have dinner before the reading. I told him about the party and Cooper's light show. "He said you had to be stoned to really appreciate it."

"That's nonsense! Did you——"

"I just had a little, Dad."

"Rob, you know, the worst reason to do anything is just because everyone else is."

"I know! That wasn't why I did it."

"Was Hope there?"

"Yeah, I think she had a good time."

There was a pause.

"Um, Dad, I was just wondering.... Are Helen and Nina coming tomorrow?"

"Yes, they've been looking forward to it."

"Oh."

"Is that all right?" He sounded slightly annoyed.

"Well, it's just...I don't think Mom would want to come if they do."

"That's up to her."

"Yeah."

"Let's make it a nice evening, sweetie, okay? It's Vanessa's night."

I hung up, feeling bad. I'd been hoping Dad would say "Helen who?" or "Why on earth should I bring *her?*"

At dinner I said I'd spoken to Dad. "He's bringing Helen and her daughter," I said, not looking right at Mom.

"Who's her daughter?" Vanessa asked.

"She has this daughter, Nina," I said. "About my age."

"Well," Mom said. "I guess that solves *that* problem."

"What problem?" Steve asked.

"I'll hear V read some other time, that's all."

"Mom, that's silly," Vanessa said. "So, she's coming. So what?"

"Why should I put myself through that kind of experience?" Mom said.

"I'm going to call Dad up and tell him not to bring her," Lowell said.

"No!" Mom cried. Then in a quieter voice, she said, "Don't say anything. It'll just make it worse."

"Why should *she* come?" Lowell said. "She's not a member of our family."

"Joel wants her there," Mom said stonily. "It's his choice."

"If he knew you wouldn't come because she was there, he wouldn't bring her," Lowell said.

I knew that wasn't true because Dad did know that.

"Her daughter writes poetry," I said, just to say anything.

No one said anything.

"Look, V, I'll hear you read dozens of times," Mom said. "This is only one time."

"It's okay with me," Vanessa said. "I just think it's cowardly not to face her. You're making it into a big deal by not coming."

"Well, it *is* a big deal to me," Mom said, her voice shaking. "It's a big deal to me that my husband is off with some other woman...showing her off in front of the family. That *is* a big deal to me. Shouldn't it be?"

"Maybe we should all not go," Lowell said, "as a protest."

"Thanks a lot," Vanessa said wryly.

"It's Dad's fault," Lowell said. "*He's* wrecking it....Call him up and tell him you won't read if he brings her."

Vanessa put her head to one side. "Lowell, come on! How can I do that? Dad's a free agent. He can do what he wants."

"Well, if it were me," Lowell said, "that's what *I'd* do."

"V has been looking forward to this for a long time," Mom said.

"So?"

"It's not that," Vanessa said. "I just don't think it's fair to Dad to have the whole family jumping on him. All of this isn't easy for him either.... And he's not coming home just because we put some ultimatum on him."

"Well, *I'm* not going," Lowell said.

"Go, sweetie," Mom said. "Really. V's right.... Joel has to do whatever——"

"She's such a dope!" Lowell said savagely. "Why'd he pick someone like her?"

I was really surprised because whenever I've tried to talk to him about it, Lowell's made it seem like I was exaggerating everything.

"Helen's not so bad," Mom said limply. "She's beautiful. Who knows?"

I didn't know what to do. I really wanted to go to Vanessa's reading, especially since she was reading that poem about me. After dinner I said to Mom, "Mom, will you mind if I go? I won't if you don't want."

"Go, hon, really.... We're making too big a thing out of this."

Later that evening Mason called.

"I was wondering if you felt like doing something tomorrow night. You know, like maybe going to the movies?"

I cleared my throat. "I'd like to.... Only the thing is, my sister has this poetry reading in the city and we're all going to go."

"Is she reading her own stuff?"

"Yeah....She's going to read a poem about me."

"Maybe another night?"

"Sure."

"You know, Robin, I just wanted to say...I guess I acted kind of dumb the other night, the way I kept staring at you?"

"Well, I did it too."

"You looked so pretty...."

"That's okay."

"I don't go away to school for two more weeks...so maybe we can get together."

"Okay."

There was a pause.

"My mother's coming home."

"You mean, for good?"

"I don't know....Dad didn't say. He just said she'd be here and they'd see how it went."

Talk about families makes me nervous.

I wore a dress to Vanessa's poetry reading. She was wearing that long, dark-red dress she wore to the party. Steve just wore a plaid shirt and jeans. He seemed more nervous than Vanessa. He drove us to the city in his car. I sat in the back seat since there were two bucket seats in front.

"Are you nervous?" I asked Vanessa.

"Very....Steve, please don't drive so fast. I'll be a basket case anyhow."

"I'm a good driver," Steve said. "Leave the driving to me, okay?"

"I just meant, we have plenty of time.... We don't need to break any records."

"I hope it's okay that I'm coming," I said. It's hard talking to the backs of peoples' necks.

"Of course it is!" Vanessa said.

"Well, but Lowell——"

"He should've come and so should Mom," Vanessa said. "She's hypersensitive."

"Look, if your husband had another woman in his life, wouldn't you——" Steve began.

"No," Vanessa said. "I'd face her down. I don't believe in jealousy anyway. It's demeaning."

"Okay, I'm glad I know that," Steve said. "I've been meaning to mention that Rochelle and I——"

"Will you shut up and drive?" Vanessa said.

"I'm very jealous," I said. "I don't blame Mom at all."

"I'm very jealous too," Steve said.

"It's just a form of insecurity," Vanessa said.

When we got to Giorgio's Dad and Helen and Nina were already there. Steve let us out and went to look for a parking space.

Horrible Helen looked really sexy. She was wearing this black dress which was high in front, but had almost no back, the kind of dress somewhat flat-chested people wear to look sexy. I mean, I guess if their breasts don't amount to much, they have to show something to get men interested. It was more the whole thing, though. Her hair was swept up in this kind of chignon and she had little pearl earrings on, the dangling kind. She looked sparkling and soft, like someone in an ad for something expensive. Dad looked regular in a seersucker suit and Nina was in green jeans and a nice striped shirt.

"Don't you look elegant!" Helen said to Vanessa and me as we sat down. "Look at them, Joel! Did you know you had two such glamorous daughters?"

"I always suspected it," Dad said, smiling at us affectionately.

We all looked at our menus. I suddenly didn't feel that hungry.

"Let's get champagne, okay?" Dad said. He seemed in a very relaxed, expansive mood.

"I don't know," Vanessa said.

"Look, is it every night I have a daughter reading her own poetry aloud?" Dad said.

"I guess a little couldn't hurt," Vanessa said. "Maybe it'll make me feel more relaxed."

"Are you nervous?" Helen said. "*I* would be."

"Well, I'm prepared," Vanessa said. "It's just——" She looked around for Steve, who hadn't come back yet. "I guess with Steve in the audience, I want to do really well. He's been coaching me."

Helen looked at Nina. "Nina, do you want to show Vanessa your poems?"

Nina shrugged.

"Nina wrote three poems which won a prize at her school this year," Helen said. "She thought you might be able to give her some criticism about them, Vanessa."

"Sure, I'd love to," Vanessa said. "Not right now, though....Could you take them, Rob?"

I put Nina's poems in my purse.

"They're not that good," she muttered to me.

"They are, darling!" Helen said. "Don't be modest....Nina's teacher couldn't believe she'd done them all by herself. He kept thinking I'd helped her. As though I could! I couldn't write a line of poetry to save myself."

Steve came in and sat down next to Vanessa. The waiter came to take our order. I ordered steak because that's something that usually tastes good, even if you're not hungry. Nina ordered brains!

I looked at her. I once saw brains in the supermarket when I was shopping with Mom. They were this horribly gooshy mass of white things, like a whole nest of worms locked together.

"They're good," she said, grinning. "You can try some, if you want."

"No, thanks!"

Somehow the whole dinner was sort of awkward. Dad and Helen kept drinking champagne and making toasts and acting all excited and happy. I felt bad. I felt like I ought to try and act cheerful for Vanessa's sake, but I didn't feel that way at all. I thought of Mom and Lowell at home and even the steak didn't taste that good.

"Did you ever get drunk?" Nina asked me.

"I don't think so," I said.

"Me neither.... But I love the way champagne tastes."

"Yeah." I tried to sip some, but it just tasted funny.

Before we had dessert Vanessa got up and said she wanted to go back and get in the mood for her reading. By then the restaurant had filled up quite a bit. There weren't a huge number of people, but about half the tables were taken. I wondered if most of them were people who especially liked poetry or if they just happened to be there for dinner. Steve went backstage with Vanessa.

"Is he your sister's boy friend?" Nina asked me.

"Yeah.... Well, he's her teacher really, but they got to know each other. He's married, but he's getting a divorce."

"Is she going to marry him?"

I shrugged.

"They're so young," Helen said.

"Well, he's certainly an improvement on some of V's other swains," Dad said.

Helen laughed and touched his hand. "Swains! Joel, what an expression."

"Beaus? What do they call them nowadays?"

"Vanessa wants to do a lot of things before she gets married," I said. "She's going to publish lots of books and things like that."

"I'm not ever going to get married," Nina said.

"Oh, honey," Helen said. "Sure you are! Everybody does."

"Everybody does *not*," Nina said fiercely.

"I don't know if I am either," I admitted.

"I think you girls are a little young to be making your mind up about all that," Dad said.

"No, we're not," Nina and I said in unison.

"Oh, I was *just* like that," Helen said. "But you fall in love with someone, darling, and then everything changes."

"Yeah?" Nina said, seeming unconvinced. "Maybe."

I like Nina. I have the feeling she isn't too crazy about her mother either.

Vanessa came out to read her poems. The restaurant was pretty dark, but they had a spotlight on her. She'd memorized all these poems, but had them in a pile on a table, just in case. It's hard to describe what it was like. I haven't heard that many people read their poetry and Vanessa is my sister so I can't be that objective. She seemed really nervous; that surprised me. Vanessa just isn't the nervous type. Once she had to stop in the middle and get the sheet her poem was written on. Another time she said the wrong word twice! She laughed and said she was sorry, but it was embarrassing. Then she came to the poem about me. She looked right over at our table and said, "This next poem is for my sister, Robin. I wrote it when she was little and she's a completely different person to me now, but I wanted to capture the way she seemed to be then, when she was eight, seven summers ago."

FOR ROBIN

Look at you
Standing alone on the sidewalk.
A chocolate kiss
Melting in the sun.
A baby lioness
Only first learning to pounce.

Glorious in the daytime
You have captured me
And set me up like a bowling pin.
For you words run together
And apart like hesitant rivers.
Your smile is heat;
A solid tree-trunk of preservation.
I can only choose to walk around
Your wide, wide shadow.

Your flower is a tiger lily.
I would pick one for you.
It is only fair
For you have given me summertime.

You are the ball
To knock down my pin.
Laughing, we both collapse
Into each other's rivers.

I felt funny while Vanessa was reading the poem about me, as though everyone was staring at me. Nina leaned over and whispered, "That was pretty!" I nodded. I looked over at Dad and he smiled at me. Helen was gazing off into space, like she wasn't listening.

Then Vanessa read some more poems. A few were love poems. I guess they were about Steve. He didn't seem to mind. He sat off to one side, staring at her every second. When she finished, a lot of people clapped. A few of them went over to Vanessa and started talking to her. I don't know if they were people she knew or what.

"You must be terribly proud, Joel," Helen said, smiling at him.

Dad looked in a kind of daze. "Yes, I..."

Nina stood up. "I have to go to the bathroom," she said.

"Me, too," I said. I'd waited all through Vanessa's reading.

It was a small bathroom. I waited while Nina went into the cubicle first. I looked at myself in the mirror. My hair looked funny. I'd washed it that morning, but it was standing out in curls all over my head.

After I came out, we stood there a minute. Nina started brushing her hair. She looked at me and smiled in an awkward way. "Well, I guess it looks like we might be stepsisters," she said wryly.

I stared at her. I felt like someone had socked me in the stomach as hard as they could. "What do you mean?"

Nina had a funny expression. "I just meant ...Well, they seem to be getting kind of serious about each other."

My heart was beating so fast I thought I was going to faint. "How can you tell?"

Nina lowered her voice, even though no one was around to hear. "Well, she lets him stay over and she doesn't do that unless it's sort of serious. And she keeps talking about how we might have to move to a bigger apartment if anything happens so I can still have my own room." She put her head to one side. "It's nothing against you," she said earnestly. "I'm just used to my own room, that's all."

"Me too," I said softly; my mouth felt all dry. I didn't know what to say.

"I like your Dad," Nina said hesitantly. "He's really nice. He's sort of sexy in a polite way. I mean, I can see what Mom sees in him. Some of the weirdos she's brought home, you wouldn't *believe*!"

"Does she say she's, um, in love with him?" I said, almost choking on the words.

"I forget," Nina said. "She said he was a witty, sensitive, adorable man. I think that's what it was."

How sick! I can't believe it. "He sleeps over?" I said, frowning. "A lot?"

"Just sometimes.... You know how they always think it'll have a traumatic effect on the kids? No, I guess you don't know since your— well, anyway, he did last Sunday and at breakfast they were both hemming and hawing. I don't care. What difference is it to *me* if he sleeps over or not? I mean, she's got to have a sex life."

The awful thing was I couldn't bring myself to hate Nina, despite her being the bearer of such hideous news. She's really sort of nice; she can't help her mother. But I felt like I wanted to die. I don't think I've ever felt so awful in my life.

When we got back to their table, Dad was sitting there by himself. He said Helen had seen someone she knew and had gone over to say hello to them. I stood there, staring at him. I was afraid I was going to burst into tears.

"Are you okay, honey?" Dad said, evidently noticing my expression. "Did something happen?"

I opened my mouth to say something, but no words came out.

Dad got up. "Let's go outside and talk," he said, taking me by the arm.

Outside it was cool and dark. I threw myself in his arms and burst into tears. I just couldn't help it. I felt like my heart was breaking.

Dad kept patting me on the shoulder. "Sweetheart, what *is* it?" he said intensely. "Tell me! Please."

"It's Nina," I gasped. "She said you're—you're going to marry her mother and she's looking at apartments already and we'll be stepsisters! ...Oh, Daddy, don't! Please don't! I can't stand it! I don't want a stepsister. I hate Helen Becker. She's horrible. Please don't do it. Please?"

Dad held me tight. "Darling, listen to me....Nothing's going to happen. Nina's got the whole thing way out of proportion."

I swallowed. "She says you sleep over there," I said accusingly.

"A couple of times, that's all."

"You shouldn't have," I said angrily. "Why did you?"

"Rob, will you listen to me for one minute? I am not going to marry Helen. Okay? I'm involved with her, she's involved with me. It's complicated. These things always are. But there are no plans for divorce or remarriage. None."

"Really?"

"Really."

I stared at him. I knew I looked awful. My eye makeup must have smeared all over the place. "Daddy?" I said softly.

"What, darling?"

"Can't you come home again? Are you afraid Mom will start yelling at you or what?"

He hesitated. "It's complicated."

"Mom wants you to come back," I said urgently. "I know she does."

"How do you know that?"

"Well, you know Ogden Haynes?"

"Sure."

"Well, Mom's been seeing him, sort of going

out on dates? Not real dates, just out, just to the movies and stuff?"

"Yes?"

"And he told Mason Mom was still in love with you."

Dad stood for a long time staring at me pensively. He sighed. "Oh, God," he said.

"Do you think you might?" I said. "Come back, I mean?"

"I want to," he said. "I want us all to be together as a family again."

"Mom's courses are going really well," I said, trying to sound cheerful. I told him how the teacher had said her stuff was so good. "I think she's, well, in a much better mood."

"Good," Dad said in a somewhat noncommittal way. "I'm glad to hear that." He put his arm around me. "I'm really glad we talked about all of this," he said. "It's very important for me to feel you can always tell me what you really feel. Will you remember that?"

I nodded.

He smiled, but in a sad way. "Sometimes I think you're the only still point in the turning world."

"What does that mean?"

"It's from a poem. I'll show it to you sometime. It means—something you can count on. Something that doesn't change."

"*I* change."

"Yes, but not...your inner essence. That remains the same. I think it would break my heart if that changed."

We stood gazing at each other. I reached over and kissed him. "I love you, Daddy."

"I love you, darling, more than I can say."

I felt sort of exhausted at that point. When we went inside, Helen was back at the table. "I think we'd better make it a night," she said to Dad. "Nina's feeling a little tired."

Dad went over to check if Vanessa and Steve were ready to leave. They said they were.

Thirteen

GOING HOME, I lay down in the back seat of the car. There wasn't a pillow, but I rolled my coat into a ball and lay down on that. I started falling asleep.

"I feel so awful," Vanessa started saying. Her voice was soft, almost a whisper.

"It wasn't bad, V, really," Steve said consolingly.

"It was! I don't know what got into me. My mouth was so dry, I could hardly speak. I felt like my lips were glued together."

He was silent a moment. "It was a difficult situation."

"Lowell was right," Vanessa said. "We all should have stayed home....I don't want to read her daughter's poems, Steve!"

"Don't, then."

"I have them," I murmured sleepily. "I put them in my bag."

Vanessa turned around. "Are you awake, Rob?"

"Half."

"Was I awful? Tell me."

"You seemed a little nervous." I still had my eyes shut.

"V, listen to me," Steve said. "You'll read lots of times. This is just once....So, you muffed it a little. Half of them didn't even notice. Look at that guy who thought you were so terrific."

"He was a fool."

"Something came across....Maybe I shouldn't have been there. Maybe that made it harder."

"No, it wasn't that." She sighed. After a second she said quietly, almost to herself, "I kept thinking of Mom and Lowell at home alone.... We had such a nice family once, really we did."

"We still do," I said.

"Oh, Robby!" Vanessa said.

"We do."

"Everything's disintegrating, falling apart."

Steve put his arm around her. "You're tired, sweetie."

They stopped talking after that or maybe I

just fell asleep. I dreamt something about a party. I was there, all dressed up, dancing with Mason and then suddenly he had to leave, something about his mother, and I didn't know how to get home. I kept going down the wrong street and making the wrong turn. The houses looked liked our house, but they would turn out to have the wrong number.

When we got home, I staggered up to bed, my eyes still half-closed. I didn't even bother taking my clothes off or anything. I just crawled under the covers and pulled them up high to my chin and fell sound, sound asleep.

I don't know what woke me up. Maybe it was just that I suddenly felt very thirsty. I hadn't had anything to drink with dinner except the champagne. I peered at my clock. It was two-twenty. I had no idea when we'd gotten home or how long I'd been sleeping. The house was totally silent. Everyone must have been asleep.

I decided to go downstairs and have some juice.

On the way downstairs, I glanced into the living room. I almost flipped. This is what I saw. Ogden Haynes was sitting on the living room couch, his feet up on the coffee table. Mom was sitting next to him, her head resting on his shoulder, her legs tucked up under her. There were two glasses of something like brandy on the table in front of them.

Suddenly Mom waved her hand out and intoned in a melodramatic way, "Hypocrisy, thy name is Helen!"

"She brought her daughter?" Ogden said, looking at her.

"But of course! Trying out for the little family bit. Shit! That woman! If I had one dollar for every time she came up to me and went into this spiel about how wonderful it was to see a marriage where both partners were 'free, open people.' She used to drag into the kitchen after Joel and watch him cook and spew out all this garbage about what a wonderful, liberated husband he was. Where were my brains? In my ass?"

"You don't know it's an affair," Ogden said.

Mom snorted. "What is it then—a three-ring circus?"

"He may just want commiseration."

"Sure....Look, I know Helen. She has a fantastic figure—slim hipped, no behind. You know, the kind of figures girls from Illinois have."

Ogden laughed. "I don't, I'm sorry. I never—"

"She is out for blood! And poor dopey Joel! Is he really going to let her tie him up and work her evil ways with him?"

"Maybe for a summer fling. I can't see it turning into much else."

"I don't know....He's the type that'll be so guilty, he'll marry her just so he won't sully her name or something."

"Hope, you know what I think?" Ogden said.

"What?"

"I think he loves you."

"Oh, love!" Mom looked exasperated. "What's that?"

"It's more than a summer fling. It's all those years of——"

"Oh, Og! What? Devotion, sharing, all that crap?"

"Why do you call it crap?"

"I've become a raving beast!" Mom said glumly.

"No, you haven't."

"I have. You don't know. You don't live with me."

"Hope, listen. I know you pretty damn well. You're going through a hard time. But you're a warm, wonderful, honest, responsive person and if Joel doesn't see that, he——"

There were a few moments of silence.

"Maybe," Mom said, sounding unconvinced. "What about June?"

"We'll see," he said.

"She seemed better, you thought?"

"Yeah, I don't know....She's always better when she's about to come home, but she said one thing that impressed me. She said, 'I have to figure out what went wrong on my own and then do something about it and there isn't a doctor on the face of the earth who can do that for me. It's up to me.'"

"She's right," Mom said. "God, I hope she makes it."

"Well, you can imagine how *I* feel. I can't even say hope. I've been up and down so many times with her, I don't know."

They were silent again.

"Why is life like this?" Mom said suddenly.

He laughed. "I don't know...I sometimes wonder.... Well, it's idle to speculate, I guess."

"What?" Mom looked down at him.

"How do you think we—do you think *we* could have made it together?"

Mom looked thoughtful. "I don't know."

"I used to watch you at parties," he said in this sort of wistful voice. "Remember when you used to wear your hair in that braid?"

"Yeah."

"You always reminded me of the heroine of a Russian short story. Well!"

Mom put her hand to his forehead. "We're going to be happy," she said. "We deserve it."

"We do."

Then she leaned over and kissed him right on the lips! They kissed for a long time. I was scared what would happen next.

"I love you," he said softly.

"I love you too," Mom said, also softly. "But——"

"Sure. I know. I just wanted to say it."

"Right."

Trying to move as quietly as I could, I went back upstairs. Wow, what a summer! Everything is topsy-turvy. Mom and Ogden Haynes love each other?

I did a peculiar thing. I just felt I didn't want to sleep by myself so I took my sleeping bag and dragged it quietly into Lowell's room. I moved it as quietly as I could, rolling it out in one corner, a few feet from his bed. He seemed to be sound asleep, his glasses resting on the night table. At night he has to wear this weird brace on his teeth. It goes all around his head and makes him look like something out of Star Trek.

"Rob?"

"Yeah?" I whispered.

"What are you doing in here?"

I hesitated. "I just couldn't fall asleep so I though maybe I'd sleep in here....Is that okay?"

"Sure." He groped for his glasses. "What time is it?"

"Late."

He looked at his clock. "Almost three."

"Yeah."

He half sat up and yawned. "So, how'd it go?"

"The reading? Kind of a mess."

"How come?"

"V was awful! She kept messing things up, forgetting lines....I don't even know if she's a good poet! The poems just sounded...funny."

"How was Dad?"

"Low, it was all...He ordered champagne and no one was in a good mood except Helen and she kept pawing at him. None of it's my imagination. You're wrong! Her daughter said she's planning the *wedding*!"

Lowell was silent.

"I got kind of hysterical. I went outside with Dad and I started crying and he said it wasn't that bad and that he had no plans to..." I started choking up again. "He sleeps *over* there! Nina said so."

"Well, lots of people get divorced," Lowell said.

"What?" I couldn't believe it. "What do you mean?"

"Well, it happens."

"So, you're just, you're just accepting it! You don't even care!"

"Rob, calm down....Of course I care....But it's their lives."

"It's our lives too."

"If they don't love each other anymore, what's the point of their getting back together? Just so they can scream at each other for the next twenty years?"

"It wouldn't *be* like that," I said breathlessly. I was having trouble talking. "Low, please don't give up on it."

"I'm not."

"I think you're wrong....I think he's realizing what a dumbo she is."

"Sure." I had the feeling Lowell was half asleep, that he wasn't even listening to me. For a while I just sat there, listening to his even breathing. Then I decided to go downstairs. Instead of tip-toeing down, I went down with loud, clumping steps so that if Mom and Ogden were in the middle of doing something, they'd have time to stop.

They weren't. The living room was completely empty.

I went into the kitchen. Mom was sitting at the kitchen table, having a cup of tea and reading an old copy of the *New Yorker*. "Hi, hon," she said. "What're you doing up?"

"I felt thirsty," I explained. I opened the refrigerator door and peered in.

"There's some cider left, if you like."

I poured myself a big mug of cider. "How come *you're* up?" I asked innocently.

"Ogden and I went out for a drive," Mom said, "and then he came back and we got to talking....He's such a good person to talk to! I feel like I wouldn't have gotten through this summer without him."

"Maybe you could marry him," I said.

Mom laughed. "I thought I *was* married."

I blushed. "I mean, just in case..."

Mom looked at me thoughtfully.

"Don't tell me about it, okay?"

"Okay."

"Ogden's a wonderful friend," Mom said. "But..."

"I bet you wish he had another name!"

Mom smiled. "I don't mind his name." She stared at me pensively. "Did it upset you, the whole thing, Dad's bringing her?"

I nodded.

"Did V do all right?"

"She was nervous....I think Helen was too. It was funny. Like she knew she didn't belong there."

I wanted to tell Mom everything, about all that Nina had said, but I knew I couldn't.

"He has to get it out of his system," Mom said suddenly.

"Why her, though?"

Mom shrugged. "Helen? She's bright, she's pretty, she's crazy about him....What man is going to turn that down?"

"But he said——" I stopped.

"What?" Mom looked wary.

"He said he wasn't going to marry her."

Mom laughed mirthlessly. "Poor Helen, in that case. Should I feel sorry for her?"

I smiled. "If you want."

Mom sipped some more of her tea. "I don't know. The milk of human kindness runs thick and fast in my veins, but not *that* thick and fast. She'll bounce back. She's the type that always lands on her feet."

"Are *you* that type?" I said, curious.

"Me?" Mom thought a minute. "Yeah, I guess I am. Joel always had an attraction to bouncy, tough creatures with a gleam in their eye. I always envisioned him with dreamy, ethereal girls, but he never liked them."

"I think I like Mason," I said. "He said he'd call tomorrow."

"Just don't rush it, hon."

"I'm not!"

"It can be something fun for the summer.... Don't try to force it into more than it is."

"Mom?"

"Yeah?"

"Who was...you know that boy you liked in college before you met Dad?"

"Scott? He was someone I'd grown up with. He lived in our apartment building. His father and Grandma used to play chess in the park. They'd come over for Thanksgiving—all his relatives were in Poland. It was like family....And when I got to college, I was so lonely, I couldn't stand it, and there he was....That's what I mean, Rob. I tried to make it into more than it was because I needed more. But it wasn't."

"And then you met Dad?"

She nodded, looking wistful.

"Mom? Do you still believe in all that—true love and stuff?"

She was silent a moment. "Yeah, I do....I don't believe it always lasts forever and I know there are no guarantees, but I think people need each other and help each other make life more...bearable."

"Did Dad do that for you?" I couldn't help asking.

She nodded. "Rob, listen, I don't regret marrying Dad. I regret marrying too young and not having continued with my art and maybe moving out here, but my marriage has been good in lots and *lots* of ways. Joel's a good, decent, caring person."

"So you loved each other?" I pressed on.

"We love each other right this second," Mom said intensely; there were tears in her eyes. "How could we not? All those years, the three of you. There's so much we've been through together."

"But people still get divorced," I said.

"I know.... Look, I don't *know* what will happen. But you don't wake up one morning and find that twenty years of love have flown clear out the window. It just doesn't work that way." She smiled. "Listen, it's three o'clock. You better get some sleep."

"You better," I said.

"We both better."

We went upstairs together.

Fourteen

"HOW ABOUT this afternoon?" Mason asked.

I hesitated. "I usually play tennis with my brother then.... Do you know how to play?"

"Reasonably.... I tried out for the tennis team at school, but didn't make it."

"Well, that's good," I said. "Neither of *us* would've made it either."

"Why don't we try the north courts? They're usually free. And if not, we can sit under a tree and talk."

If Mason even tried *out* for the tennis team, that probably means he's a lot better than Lowell and me, but still, I guess it doesn't matter so much. I spent the morning looking over my tennis outfits. When I play with Lowell, I just wear cutoff shorts and a t-shirt, but this time I decided to wear this yellow tennis dress Terry passed on to me. Her aunt got it for her, at a fancy New York tennis store, and she couldn't exchange it because all they had was other tennis things. Terry is not exactly the athletic type.

Later in the morning Grandma called.

"Oh hi, Granny....I was meaning to call you. We were going to come in last week, but things have been kind of busy here. Vanessa's boy friend arrived and she gave this poetry reading."

"Jacob and I would have loved to come," Grandma said, sounding hurt.

"Granny, it was kind of a mess," I said. "I can't explain, but..."

"So, when will I see you? It's been so long."

"I don't know."

"Jump on a bus this afternoon! You can be here by supper."

"I can't, Granny....See, I met this boy? He used to go to school with me and then he transferred. Only we ran into each other again and we set up this tennis match for this afternoon, Lowell and him and me."

"Perfect!" Grandma exclaimed. "I'll bring my new racket and beat the pants off all three of you. Did I tell you I got a Prince?"

"Uh uh."

"It's unfair, but what a racket! I'll let you try it, Robbie, and if you like it, maybe we'll get you one for your birthday."

"But Jacob doesn't play, does he?" I said.

"He'll umpire. He loves to watch tennis. He says it's like ballet. He keeps me from cheating."

"I guess we could play doubles," I said hesitantly. "I never played with Mason before. I don't know how good he is."

"What time is it set up for?"

"Three....He's picking us up."

"Terrific....I've missed you terribly, darling. What's with the home scene?"

"Well, it's...We'll talk when you get here, Granny, okay?"

When I hung up, I felt funny. Here I'd been looking forward to a quiet afternoon alone with Mason and now it had escalated to a foursome with Grandma and Lowell and Jacob! It wasn't that I didn't want to see Grandma again, but I'd imagined it all differently.

I got into the yellow tennis dress and tied my hair back in a ponytail. Mom was in the den, working. I told her about Grandma and Jacob coming out for the afternoon.

Mom made a face. "Are they staying over?"

"She didn't say."

"Shit, I'm inundated with work, Rob. Couldn't you stop her?"

"She said she missed us and she hasn't seen us in so long."

Mom sighed. "Listen, I'm leaving it all up to

you, okay? You and Lowell. Keep her out of my hair or I may commit some indecent act."

Grandma came driving up in her Chrysler at around three. She usually does the driving since Jacob's eyesight isn't that good. He drove until about two years ago when his doctor said he ought to stop. He hugged me.

"How's your new cello bow, Jacob?" I asked him.

"Beautiful....It's so beautiful. I just look at it every morning...with reverence."

"Give it my love."

Grandma's tennis dress was white with a pocket on one side for the ball. One thing about Grandma's game is that she never double-faults. Her serve isn't that hard, but it always lands in exactly the same place.

"Mason, this is my Grandma," I said. He'd arrived earlier and I'd explained to him about how the whole thing had gotten set up.

"I think we can take on these two light-weights, don't you?" Grandma said, winking at Mason.

"Sure," Mason said. "I like your racket, Mrs. Herskowitz."

"Liz."

As we divided up to go to our sides of the court, I whispered to Lowell, "Let's let them win, okay?"

"Why?"

"Well, it'll make Grandma feel good."

"Don't be silly.... We'll just play our usual game."

About halfway through the first set it became clear that even if Lowell and I had played our best, we'd have a hard time winning. Grandma can't run too fast, but when the ball comes to her, she really wallops it. And Mason was one of those people who, without seeming to move that fast, cover the whole court.

"Forget what I said," I said to Lowell when we were behind four games to one. "Let's really play to win."

He laughed. "What do you *think* I'm doing?"

"Well, play back on my serve! I can't cover the whole backcourt."

"Then we won't have a net game.... How're we going to get any points?"

"I don't know."

Lowell and I shouldn't have played together. We end up fighting and playing our worst. The last game ended as Grandma lobbed the ball effortlessly over both our heads; we were at the net.

"Bravo, Liz!" Jacob shouted from the bench. "Bravo!"

We sat down to rest.

"That lob has gotten me out of a lot of tight spots," Grandma admitted.

"Maybe Robin and I should play together this time," Mason said.

"Do you want to lose?" I asked him wryly.

"Why don't you try my racket, Rob?" Grandma said. "It's terrific. You can't miss."

I don't know what was wrong with me. There I was with Grandma's Prince racket and Mason on my side giving me lots of good advice about strategy and we lost anyway! It was a lot closer than it was in the first set, though.

"She's unbeatable," Jacob said proudly as Grandma sat down next to him on the bench. He looked at Mason. "What do you think of this lady, huh? Tell me honestly."

"I'm glad you could come out and play with us, Mrs.... Liz," Mason said.

"Listen, I'd come out every weekend," Grandma said. "I miss these kids like crazy."

In the car driving back to our house Lowell sat in front with Grandma and Jacob. I don't know if he did it on purpose so Mason and I could have the back seat to ourselves. We sat close together. I had tied a yellow ribbon around my ponytail to match the tennis dress. Mason reached over and touched it. Then he left his arm around my shoulder. Our legs were right next to each other. We looked at each other and smiled.

"I had a dream about you last night," he said, but softly, almost in a whisper.

"What about?"

"It was sort of strange.... You had to go to a costume party, but you couldn't find anything to wear. You were wearing this old-fashioned dress with millions of buttons down the back and you couldn't get them buttoned." He moved his hand down my shoulder to where my breast began.

"I'm sorry we lost," I whispered. "It was my fault."

"No, it wasn't. I kept staring at you....I played terribly."

Mom was carrying in some groceries when we all came back. "So you'll stay over, Mother?" she said brightly.

"We don't want to put you to too much trouble," Grandma said.

"Oh, we can just grill some fish outdoors," Mom said. "You haven't been out for so long."

"I hear you've been very busy," Grandma said, "what with the courses and all."

"Yes," Mom said. "Rob, help me, will you? Hi, Jacob....How did the tennis go?"

"Liz was victorious, as always," Jacob said. "What can you expect?"

"Joel's in the city," Mom said, bustling around the kitchen. "Did you hear? He's getting a lot of work done on his novel."

"Where's he staying?" Grandma asked, pretending this was the first she'd heard of it.

"Leo Meister's place....You remember him, Mother, don't you? He teaches art history at Columbia. He's over in Rome for the summer."

"Ah Rome!" Jacob said. "Remember our October in Rome, Liz?"

"How could I forget?"

"Was that on your honeymoon?" Mason asked.

They both smiled.

"I call it our honeymoon," Jacob said.

I took Mason aside and explained that Grandma and Jacob weren't married. "They like each other a lot, though."

Jacob helped with the dinner. He set the grill going outdoors and appointed me his assistant. "With fish, moistness is everything," he said. "A touch of spices, a quick grazing over the fire and there you have it....No heavy sauces. It's like Bach, simple, perfect."

We ate outside while the light faded. I had a little of the wine Grandma had brought. It was nice, a little sweet. Lowell lit the outdoor candles.

"I'm going in to rest a little," Jacob said. "Tell me when you're ready to leave, darling."

"The poor thing," Grandma said after he'd gone in. "He can't get through an evening without his nap....We went to the opera the other night—his favorite, *The Queen of Spades*—and he fell asleep in the third act."

Mom cut herself a slice of banana cake. "So, you haven't spoken to Joel?" she asked.

"Why should I have?" Grandma said. "I had no idea he was in the city." She looked keenly at Mom. "It must be lonely for you, Hopie."

Mom shrugged.

"Are you seeing anyone?"

"Seeing anyone?" Mom sounded sarcastic.

"Dating anyone?" Grandma had a wry expression.

"No, I haven't been 'dating anyone,'" Mom said. "I was under the illusion I was married."

"Even married people," Grandma said, "sometimes——"

"Sometimes they do and sometimes they don't," Mom said. "Okay?"

"Okay," Grandma said with mock meekness.

"Mom has a very nice friend," I said. "His name is Ogden Haynes."

"That poor schlemiel?" Grandma said.

At that Mom jumped up. "It so happens that Ogden is one of the most intelligent, kind, terrific people I have met in my whole *life*. And to call a man a schlemiel who's stood by a mentally ill wife, who's raised a son while holding down a full-time job—well, if that's a loser, I'd like to know your definition of a winner!" With that she stormed into the house.

Grandma looked at Lowell and me and smiled. "You see this foot sticking out of my mouth?"

"I wondered about that," Lowell said with a smile.

"Dad says it's a cliché about redheads having terrible tempers."

"You should have seen her at two," Grandma said ruefully. She sighed.

A moment later, Mom, her cheeks bright pink, walked back onto the lawn. She sat down again.

"So, let's start a new topic," Grandma said, undaunted. "How's Joel?"

"He's fine," Mom muttered from behind the paper.

"I always liked Joel," Grandma said more or less to Lowell and me since Mom was in hiding. "He's a little immature, but so? There are worse faults."

Mom said from behind the paper, "What's immature about him?"

"It's nothing to do with him," Grandma said. "All men are immature. Right? I mean, they say in nursery school boys are way behind girls—*and* in grade school."

"But later they catch up," I said.

"Don't you believe it," Grandma said. "They never catch up. Never! Don't let anyone ever tell you they catch up."

"Lowell is mature," I said. Lowell was gazing off into space and hearing either everything or nothing. Probably everything.

"Lowell's an exception," Grandma said. "The exception that proves the rule."

Mom put down the paper. "Mother, you know this is all very well, but there *happen* to be children in the room."

"There are?" Grandma said, looking startled and looking all around. "Where? Where are they? Show me. I don't see any."

Mom pointed silently to Lowell and me.

Grandma laughed. "Them? Come off it, Hope....They know more than either of us will *ever* know. Children, my eye!"

It's hard to win an argument with Grandma.

By the time Jacob woke up from his nap, Grandma and Mom weren't speaking that much.

"Tell your mother she's got to have more of a sense of humor about life," Grandma said as she was leaving, knowing full well Mom was within earshot. "Without a sense of humor you're lost." She kissed us. "Bear up, kids! Fight the good fight!...When am I going to see you again?"

"We'll call you, Granny," I said.

"You're two darlings," Grandma said. "I don't know how they managed it, but they did."

I love Grandma. I wonder if she's right about men being immature. Sometimes I think she says things just to get Mom's goat. She usually succeeds.

Fifteen

THE WEEK Terry was due back from Europe, a really exciting thing happened. Wendy called up and asked if I could be a bridesmaid in her wedding! What happened was this. Wendy has a friend, Claudia Frank, whom she went to camp with when she was nine, ten and eleven. Then Claudia moved to California, but they still kept in touch and wrote letters back and forth. Claudia got married right in the middle of her freshman year in college. Evidently she had to—that is, she got pregnant and didn't want to have an abortion and was really in love with this boy who was the father of her baby. She wanted to come to Wendy's wedding, but she found out she's going to have another baby and her morning sickness is so bad, she can't travel at all.

"I hate to ask you at the last minute like this," Wendy said. "But it would be *such* a terrific favor, Robin. Do you think you could?"

"Sure," I said. I tried not to sound too excited, just blasé, as if I'd been to hundreds and hundreds of weddings. "How about the dress, though?"

"I think it'll fit.... Claudia's just about your size, and if not, we can pin it a little.... Oh, wouldn't you *know* something like this would happen just at the last minute? Claudia's just like that."

"Well, for me it's nice," I said. "I'm glad."

I felt pleased, too, that Wendy thought of me as a real friend, even though I'm three years younger than she is.

That afternoon I went over and tried on the dress. It isn't exactly like Vanessa's. It's the same shade of pink, but it doesn't have quite so much lace going down the front. It's a little bit low-cut.

"Sexy," Wendy said.

I swallowed. "Is that okay?" I didn't know bridesmaids were supposed to be sexy.

"I think you need another kind of bra, don't you, Mom?"

Mrs. Haskell was standing back, looking at

me. "Definitely....But the waist is nice. We don't need to do a *thing* about the hem....Oh, I could just *kill* that Claudia. Did you know she's in her third month and she didn't even tell us?"

"She must have wanted to come to the wedding a lot," I suggested.

"Someone better give that girl a good talking to," Mrs. Haskell said. "How old is the other one? Ten months?"

"She likes babies, Mom," Wendy said.

"Well, we *all* like babies," Mrs. Haskell said. "Who *doesn't* like a baby?...Oh, hon, what did you decide about cousin Sarah? Are you going to let her bring him?"

Wendy scowled. "I have to, Mom....She won't come otherwise."

Mrs. Haskell sighed. "She's our favorite cousin," she said to me. "Sarah is, and you should *see* her baby! A darling! But she's still nursing! And she wants to bring him to the ceremony. I'm just petrified she'll yank out a breast and start breast-feeding right smack while Wendy's saying 'I do.'"

"She can sit in the back," Wendy suggested in her mild voice.

"Can't these people afford baby-sitters?" Mrs. Haskell wanted to know. "Babies are wonderful in their place....But this isn't the Congo. What's wrong with bottles, for goodness' sake?"

"Cows' milk isn't as nourishing," Wendy said. "I'm going to nurse, aren't you, Robin? I think babies like it better."

"I haven't decided yet," I admitted.

"Not when they're really big," she said. "Not with teeth and all."

"That's when I quit on you, miss, I can tell you that," Mrs. Haskell said. "One day you stuck out this little row of white teeth and just nipped me. Just like that! I said, 'Baby, it's bottle time from now on.'"

Mrs. Haskell said she'd let the top part of my dress out just a bit so I wouldn't have trouble breathing and my breasts wouldn't stick out so much in front. There were only two days till the wedding, but she said she was a fast sewer. "Now, aren't I lucky I kept that old Singer up in the attic," she asked Wendy. "Your father said, 'Throw it out, use the new one, that old one's not worth a cent'....And now look: in an emergency, it does the job."

"Do I have to wear any special kind of underwear?" I said nervously.

"Just get that kind of bra I mentioned," Mrs. Haskell said.

"Do you have one of those fluffy slips?" Wendy said. "I can lend you one. It makes the dress stand out nicely." She took me up to her room. It was a real mess—things lying all over the place. "Is Vanessa still mad at me?" she said, looking through her drawer for the slip.

"Oh, she's not mad," I said. "It's just——"

"You know, it's funny," Wendy said. "Vanessa thinks I believe in marrying young. I don't! I didn't think I'd be getting married till

I was thirty! But then I met Ramsey and I figured, here's this wonderful man. What should I do? Toss him back and let some other girl snatch him up?"

"I think he's nice," I said.

"Vanessa thinks he's a male chauvinist just because he doesn't cook," Wendy said. "But, Rob, he just never learned, that's all. He *wants* to learn! He's learned how to do a chicken, he can do pork chops....He's eager to learn....But he has his father's business. Now you tell me how he's supposed to run a multi-million-dollar business supplying dental equipment to half the Midwest and run home and cook pork chops all at the same time?"

"It would be hard," I said.

Wendy handed me the slip. It was really pretty with a lace flounce and ribbons. "You know, Vanessa's my best friend, but she gets me so mad! Her and Cooper. I know what they think. They think I'm going to vegetate out there. They're so prejudiced, the both of them. What do they *know* about the Midwest? Nothing!" She glared at me. "I'm *not* going to vegetate, Rob. Really. I'm going to get my teaching degree. I'm going to do *lots* of things."

As I was leaving Mrs. Haskell called out, "You tell your mother and brother the reception's at five, okay?"

I nodded.

"Will your father be around?" Mrs. Haskell asked.

I swallowed. "I don't think so."

She smiled brightly. "Well, if he is, you tell him we'd love to have him come!"

"I will."

When I got home, I called Dad and told him I was going to be in Wendy's wedding. "Mrs. Haskell said you could come to the reception afterwards, if you like."

"Rob, I just have to hammer out this last chapter," Dad said. "It's almost Labor Day."

"I know it is!" I said, waiting for him to add more.

"But give Wendy a kiss and hug for me," was all he said.

I didn't sleep that well the night before the wedding. I kept thinking of everything; all the fights over the summer, Mom and Dad's wedding picture, walking with Mason through the grass, Cooper's light show.

In the morning I washed my face with cold water and got dressed. The wedding was at eleven. Lowell got out his camera and took some pictures of Vanessa and me.

"Steve, take some of the three of us," Vanessa said, putting Lowell between us.

Steve had a suit on; he looked more formal than I'd ever seen him.

Vanessa had given Wendy and Ramsey four books of poetry, all wrapped up in some lovely flowered paper. We went up to her room to give it to her. The room was full of bridesmaids, some cousins, some aunts. Everyone was running around screaming because Wendy couldn't find one of her earrings. "It's a present from Ramsey's mother," Wendy wailed. "She'll die if I've lost it."

Vanessa said, "Don't be silly, Wen." She hugged her. "You look lovely."

"Do you forgive me?" Wendy said.

"For what?"

"For getting married?"

"Sure I do." They hugged each other.

The wedding was out on the front lawn of Wendy's house. They have a big old-fashioned house with porches in front and in back. I walked next to Vanessa down the aisle. The slip I'd borrowed from Wendy was a little too tight, but I knew I looked pretty.

Afterward they cut the cake and everyone danced on the lawn. A man I didn't know came over to me and said, "Now, you've got to be Wendy's sister." He was tall and stocky and had a drooping blond mustache.

I shook my head.

He looked mournful. "You're *not*?"

"No...I'm Robin."

"But Sam said Wendy had a delectable sister with big green eyes whom I'd fall madly in love with the minute I saw her."

I pointed across the lawn where Wendy's sister, Nancy, was eating a piece of cake. "That's her. That's Nancy."

"No." He shook his head sadly. "I refuse to

believe it....You must be someone's sister, aren't you?"

"Yeah....My sister Vanessa is Wendy's best friend."

The man grinned. "Well there....You see. Sam was right after all....Will you dance with me, Robin?"

I laughed. I'd had a glass of champagne and I was beginning to feel good. "I'm not a very good dancer."

"Yes, you are," he said. "You're good at everything....That's why I was scared to come over to talk to you. Accomplished, dazzling young girls scare me....You go to Smith, don't you?"

I shook my head.

"Wellesley? Radcliffe?"

I made a face. "I'm just in high school. I'm a sophomore."

He struck his head. "High school!...But look at you! How can you be in high school?" He leaned toward me. "You failed gym?"

I shook my head.

"Latin?"

"Uh uh."

He sighed. "The teacher kept you back....He just couldn't bear to have you graduate....Listen, what do you mean you can't dance? You're a terrific dancer."

"I am?"

"Sure, look at you."

I looked down at my feet. "I never danced on grass before."

"Robin, I'm so glad you're not Wendy's sister. I don't want to fall in love with someone with three sisters and two brothers. I bet you're an orphan. I always luck out in things like this."

"Nope."

"Only child?"

"I have an older sister and an older brother."

He grinned at me. "It's fate! I told you it was fate. *I* have an older sister and an older brother. We were meant for each other." He held out his wrist. "Press this button, okay, Robin?"

I pressed the button on his watch.

"See.... Now look, it's now August twenty-ninth, 1981...and three o'clock and twenty-four minutes and eighteen seconds. Can you remember that?"

I nodded.

"Okay, now here's the deal. You graduate from high school and you go on...you get your law degree or whatever....I'm going to be an anthropologist. Did I mention that? Either an anthropologist or I'll do some Albert Schweitzer bit and go into the jungle and cure lepers. But you'd be bored with that, right? So, what we do is...in ten years, on August twenty-ninth, 1991...at three twenty-four, we get married."

"I don't know your name!" I giggled.

"I have a wonderful name. You'll love my name. Louis."

I shook my head. "I don't love it."

"How about Isaac? That's my middle name...."
He looked serious. "No, look, Robin, I know I'm

sounding a bit off the wall, but the thing is, I'm going to be in a jungle! And you're going to be getting your M.B.A.....So this way, we just sit back, it's all settled. Are you going to grow much taller? I'm five-ten and the men in my family don't get much taller than that."

"I don't think so."

He mopped his forehead. "Whew, I'm bushed. ...Can you imagine, I could have gotten engaged to Wendy's sister."

"Louis?"

"What?" He looked concerned.

"I think I drank too much champagne....I feel sick."

"Uh oh! Really sick? Are you going to——"

I nodded.

Louis guided me into Wendy's house. I went into the bathroom and threw up. Then I brushed my teeth with my finger and some Crest. When I came out, Louis was lying on the bed, gazing out the window.

"How is it?" he asked.

"Better."

"It was my dancing," he said sadly. "I whirled you around like a maniac." He gazed at me. "You look pale and wan...but incredibly lovely....Are you sure you're fifteen?"

I nodded.

"We could make passionate love right here in the bridal suite...except I'm so damn sleepy."

"Me too." I felt terribly, terribly sleepy. I lay

down next to him. "Are your parents divorced?" I asked him.

"Not since I last saw them." He kissed my hair. "You have wonderful crinkly hair."

"My father has a girl friend," I said, kissing him on the neck. "And she's such an awful, awful dope."

"They always are." He kept kissing me.

"I'm so scared he'll marry her."

"He won't."

"Won't he?"

"Uh uh...I promise....Robin, listen, we have to go downstairs."

"But I'm so sleepy."

"This is going to be one of those honorable moments that I'm going to spend the rest of my life regretting."

I sat up and kissed him again. "But we'll get married and do it thousands and thousands of times."

"True."

We gazed at each other.

"We used to have a dog named Isaac," I told him.

"My bark is worse than my bite."

"Let's hear it."

Louis got down on the floor on all fours and started barking. Vanessa came into the room. She was with Wendy.

"Lou!" Wendy cried. "What are you doing up here? You're supposed to be with my sister."

"I thought this *was* your sister," Louis said, getting up off the floor.

"She's *my* sister," Vanessa said, "and she's fifteen years old."

"I felt sick," I said. "I drank too much champagne."

Louis looked at Vanessa. Her hair was loose down her back. "You're beautiful too....My God, what am I going to do? Sisters, sisters everywhere!"

"You get downstairs this *minute!*" Wendy said. "Poor Nan's been spending all *afternoon* looking for you."

Louis headed for the door. He pointed to his watch. "Remember?" he said.

"He's a crazy guy," Wendy said. "You know he graduated high school at fifteen? He wants to be some kind of witch doctor and live in Africa. He's driving my aunt Irene crazy!"

"You're married!" I said, hugging her. "How does it feel?"

"I don't know. Just the same, no different yet. I better go freshen up." She went into the bathroom.

"Where's Steve?" I asked Vanessa. I still felt a little funny.

She waved her hand dismissively. "He's sitting under a tree talking about Descartes with someone's uncle, a philosophy professor....How could I fall in love with someone who doesn't even dance?"

"*I* danced," I said gaily. "I danced all over the place."

"I saw you.... What were you doing up here, Rob? My goodness, Louis is in medical school. What were you two *up* to?"

"We got engaged," I said. I felt giddy and happy.

"What?"

"Just a joke.... It's not for ten years, don't worry."

Vanessa and I wandered downstairs. It had begun clouding up. A wind was blowing across the lawn. It looked as though it might rain. Wendy's mother was sitting on the porch steps with her shoes off.

"It was a lovely wedding, Mrs. Haskell," I said as we prepared to leave.

Mrs. Haskell was holding a baby on her lap. "And he didn't cry once! Look at this fellow." She peered down at him. "Do you forgive me for all those wretched things I said about you? Do you?"

The baby grinned toothlessly up at her.

"I think he does," Vanessa said.

"I have to get used to babies again," Mrs. Haskell said. "Can't tell when I'll be a grandma."

"Wendy's finishing college," Vanessa couldn't resist saying. "She just told me."

Mrs. Haskell grinned. "Oh, well, life intervenes. You know how it is."

Vanessa snarled as we walked away.

We couldn't find Steve so we decided just to walk home.

"I guess Mom didn't feel up to the reception," Vanessa said.

"I guess not."

The house was dark and silent, except for a light on in the living room. We walked in slowly. There was Mom asleep on the couch, one arm over her eyes. She was still dressed so she must have fallen asleep while she was reading.

Vanessa knelt down to her. "Mom?" she whispered softly.

No answer.

"Poor little Mom," Vanessa said.

We went into the kitchen.

"She was tired," I said.

"Oh, Rob." Vanessa hugged me. She was crying. "I hate weddings."

Sixteen

TERRY IS BACK! She called me the same day she got in. She said she felt a little groggy from jet lag, but why didn't I come over for an hour or so just to talk.

It was really terrific seeing her again. We started being friends when we were both eight, and it seems like we've been through everything together, almost like with someone in your own family.

"I've got to show you his picture," she said, closing the door carefully.

"Who?"

"Sasha!"

"Who's he?"

"He's my boy friend. I met him in Rome." She looked really excited. Her hair was much longer than when she'd gone away, all loose and curly. "Rob, we did it!"

"You did?" I felt slightly forlorn. "How could you? I mean, what about the group you were traveling with?"

"So, they gave us free time. We stayed at a lot of these youth hostels and at night you could kind of roam around." She showed me his photo.

He was really cute, sort of the same type as Martin Darmour, curly blond hair and a terrific smile. He was in a bathing suit. "What was it like?" I asked.

She pondered. "Well, the first time it hurt."

"Horribly?"

"No, just somewhat."

Of course, one person's somewhat is another person's horribly. "So, what did you do?"

"I figured it was bound to get better after a while so I kind of gritted my teeth and stuck it out."

"Did it?"

"What?"

"Get better."

She smiled. "Oh, yeah."

"When?"

"Oh, about the sixth time or so."

I thought about this. "After it stopped hurting, was it really good or just neutral?"

"Really good!...Well, he knew what he was doing. He'd had sex with lots of girls. And, you know, I was sure he'd say I was too fat or something and he didn't! He kept saying what a beautiful Rubensesque body I had and stuff like that."

Terry is a little plump, not much, more round, kind of. She had breasts at eight! I sighed. "I think I'm going to be the last person on earth to do anything," I said.

"You didn't meet anybody all summer?"

I told her about Mason.

"Well, that's terrific," Terry exclaimed. "A weekend at his school! You're bound to do it then!"

"I don't know, he seems more the shy type."

"Well, still....He'd probably like to, if he knew you did."

"Do you think so?"

"Sure! He's probably planning it right now....When I met Sasha, I didn't know he thought of me that way at *all*. He's nineteen, and I just thought he thought of me as a kid or something....Whereas he told me later he started thinking right away about whether I'd want to have sex with him the first five minutes we met!"

I looked at the photo again. "He has a really good figure."

"I know! You know, it's funny, Rob, I always thought men's bodies looked so gross, like in *Playgirl*? But in real life they're really nice. I mean, even penises aren't so bad, once you get used to them."

I guess I have to take Terry's word for that for the time being anyway. I told her about Mom and Dad. "I just wish I knew what was going to happen," I said.

"That Helen sounds so *awful*," Terry said sympathetically.

"She is! Really gross. Totally insincere. I don't see how Dad can stand her."

I felt so much better after we had talked. Friends are a good thing.

That afternoon Mom came up to me. "Hon, I may be back a little late tonight. It's my last class and I'm going to meet Dad afterward." She looked pensive. "There's a lot we have to talk about."

My heart sank. Please don't talk about getting divorced! I must have looked anxious because she took my hand and said, "It'll be okay, honey. Don't worry."

All evening, I kept thinking of Mom and Dad being together and praying it was going well, praying they were getting along. Then I'd imagine them screaming at each other the way they did this spring and Mom coming home and saying Dad was going to stay in the city permanently.

When I was getting ready for bed, the phone rang. It was Mom.

"Rob?"

"Yeah?"

"Listen, it's gotten a little late and I think—
I think I'll stay over in the city."

"Oh."

"Is that okay? I'll be there in the morning."

"Sure."

"You have Dad's number, don't you?"

"Uh huh." I wanted to say, "How did it go?
What did you decide?" But I couldn't. I just said
good-bye and hung up. Then I raced into Lowell's room. He was reading, as usual. I grabbed
the book out of his hand.

"Hey, what're you doing?" he said. "You lost
my place."

"You'll find it again....Listen, Low, Mom
just called and she's staying in the city at Dad's
place!"

"So?"

"So, what do you think that means?"

Lowell smiled. "That they're getting back
together again and will live happily ever
after."

"Low, I *mean* it. Tell me what you really
think."

"I really think it means it got late and she
figured why not stay at his place rather than
rent a room in a hotel."

I looked at him, dismayed. "That's *all*?"

"Rob, I don't know....But why second-guess
it? You'll find out tomorrow."

"I want it to be good," I said fervently. "I want
him to come home."

"Well, sure, so do I."

I lay in bed thinking about it and finally fell asleep.

The next morning at around eleven Mom and Dad came home together. The way it happened was this. I was sitting in the kitchen, having cereal, when the door opened and there was Dad! I jumped up, ran over and hugged him.

"Where's Lowell?" he asked.

"He's at the library. I'll get him."

I bicycled down to the library, which is about ten minutes from our house. Lowell was sitting behind the front desk.

"Low, Dad's back!" I said.

Lowell smiled. "Shh, you're in the library."

"Shh? Lowell, come on! Let's go. You can take the bike. I'll walk."

"What do you mean, come on? I just got here, Rob. I'm on till two."

I felt like strangling him. "Lowell, will you get out from behind that damn desk this second? Just leave them a note."

He looked at me patiently. "Rob, I have a job.... Remember, a real honest-to-God job. I am here for a purpose. I am here to sign out books."

I pondered. "Listen, I have a great idea.... Lock the library and put a sign on the outside saying 'Will Open at Two.'"

"How about all the people who were planning to come here this morning?"

"Oh, who cares about them!"

"Hey, I just had another great idea."

"Another? What was the first one?"

"Shut up....I'll get Terry to come down and sub for you."

"Does she know the first thing about it?"

"You can show her. It can't be all *that* complicated."

"Well, as I recall, Terry isn't exactly the quickest——"

"Where's the phone?"

Terry said she could be here in five minutes. She rushed in, all excited, and listened while Lowell explained what to do. "Can I call you, if I get mixed up?" she asked.

"It's really quite simple, Terry," Lowell said, "but sure....You know our number."

Terry sat behind the desk. "Do I look official?"

I smiled. "Terrific. Thanks so much, Ter."

I let Lowell have the bike, but he said he'd walk too. "Rob, take it easy," he said, putting his hand on my arm. "He's not going to vanish into thin air, is he?"

"Maybe. How do I know?...Did she look any different?"

"Who?"

"Terry!"

"From what?"

"From when you last saw her?" I lowered my voice even though we were alone on the road. "She has a lover named Sasha....I just won-

— 213 —

dered—I mean, does she look more womanly or sensual or anything?"

"Rob, I was trying to explain card-cataloguing to her in five minutes. I wasn't checking her over for——"

"Do you think she's sexy?"

"I don't know. Kind of, I guess."

"Low, if you had to marry Terry, Sharon Darwitz or Eleanor Perkins or be shot to death, who would you pick?"

"I'd be shot to death."

"Lowell!"

At home Dad and Mom were in the living room.

"Hi, Dad," Lowell said in his infuriatingly calm way.

Dad hugged him. "How goes it, kid?"

We decided to eat lunch outside. We gathered around the wooden picnic table. Vanessa was off somewhere.

"Tell them, Joel," Mom said.

"What?" I looked anxiously at Dad who was spreading mustard on his hot-dog roll.

"It's about my novel," he said.

He explained that some editor had read it and really liked it. Liked it so much that they're going to give him something called an advance for it. That means they give you some money and if they like it, after you've made changes, they give you even more! If you figure it probably costs them a lot of money to print the book, that means they really have to like it a lot.

"I want all of you to read it," Dad said, "and give me some frank suggestions. Tell me exactly what you think."

"Straight from the shoulder, huh?" Lowell said.

Dad smiled. "It's not the Great American Novel. I'm under no illusions about that, but I'd like it to be as good as it can be."

I felt a little disappointed. It would have been nice if it *was* the Great American Novel. I'm not sure what that is exactly. Maybe something like *Moby Dick*, something really long with lots of characters.

"Look, you did it, you finished it," Mom said. "That's impressive enough."

"Did Mom mention that she got an *A* in her course?" Dad said.

Mom smiled. "Yup, he said he thought I have a lot of talent.... Not that I didn't know that already, but it's nice to have it confirmed."

That afternoon Dad went and had his novel Xeroxed and gave copies to all of us, including Vanessa who came back toward dinner. We agreed to meet at the end of the week and have a big family powwow to tell Dad what we'd thought, but that we wouldn't talk among each other till then.

I was so excited to read Dad's novel that the minute I got it, I went off and sat down in a quiet place in the yard. I read the whole thing without stopping. I think it was what you'd call an autobiographical novel. At least the main character sounded and looked quite a bit like Dad. His name was Willard. I wonder why Dad picked such a funny name! It reminded me of that movie about the man who trained rats to kill people.

The beginning part about Dad's (Willard's) childhood wasn't so interesting. It got good when he met Mom. I guess I might not have known it *was* Mom so much if Lowell hadn't told me that story about how they met. Willard sees this girl, Sophie, in a coffee shop and gets a crush on her, only he's too scared to say anything because she's always with another boy. "He could tell from her warm animated smile and winsome manner that she knew men liked her," he says. I'm not exactly sure what "winsome" means; I guess perky or something.

Then there was that part Lowell described about when they had sex for the first time. It said, "He had never imagined anyone could look so beautiful." You could tell that was Mom because he said her pubic hair was carrot red, just like her regular hair. That's true. I've seen Mom naked so I know. It also said Willard was fascinated by the freckles she had under her left breast. I never knew *that*! I suppose I've never looked under Mom's left breast!

The next part, about how Willard was trying to decide whether to be an architect or just go to Paris to paint, was sort of dull; I skimmed through that. But the last part, which Dad was in the middle of, got interesting again. Willard and Sophie had gotten married. They had two children, a boy and a girl. The boy was named James and Dad described him as "calmly perceptive"; the girl, who was named Erin, seemed like a combination of me and Vanessa.

What he said about the girl, Erin, was really nice. "When he saw her serious, lovely face as she sat cross-legged in front of her doll house, he felt that all the things he had first loved in Sophie were rekindled." He described this game we used to play where I'd hide under the covers or in the closet and he'd look for me. "At the thought of her growing up, of losing her, he felt a pain in his heart, abashed though he was to admit it, even to himself. He wanted her to be happy and free, yet he wanted her never to leave. Luckily, like all children, she would do what she wanted."

Sunday morning we all met in the den to talk about it.

"I liked it, Dad," Lowell said. He was sitting cross-legged on the floor in bare feet. "Of course, I don't read novels that much so it's hard for me to compare....I guess I thought the beginning was a little dull."

"That's what the editor said," Dad said. He was taking notes on a yellow lined pad.

"I kind of wished the brother had had a more major role," Lowell said. "I mean, let's face it, he *was* the wittiest character in the book and when he wasn't there, the plot kind of——"

"I'll take that into consideration," Dad said with a smile.

"How about you, Robin?" Dad said. I was sitting right next to Lowell.

"Well, I liked it a lot too," I said hesitantly. "I think——"

"Oh, Dad," Lowell said. "You got that thing wrong about the brother, that time he tries out for the baseball team? You said——"

"Low, let Robin finish, okay?" Dad said.

"I liked the part at college," I said hesitantly, "where he meets Sophie."

"The dirty parts especially," Lowell said, raising his eyebrows.

"Lowell! They were *not* dirty," I said.

"Hey Dad, I have a great idea," Lowell went on. "Why don't you let *me* write some dirty scenes for you?"

"*You?*" I said.

"Yeah, it's easy. You just get a bunch of bestsellers and copy what they do."

"That is a truly gross idea," I said.

"I think I'll let well enough alone, Low," Dad said dryly.

"Okay," Lowell said. "I just thought you might want to make some money, but I guess not."

"Sex scenes written by *you* wouldn't make money for anyone," I said.

"Wanna bet?"

"Kids," Dad said. "Cool it, will you?" He looked at Vanessa, who had been sitting coolly and imperiously in her Japanese kimono, listening. "V?"

"It's hard for me to be objective," she said.

"I know that, darling."

"It has some lovely things in it." She looked contemplative. "But the present tense is a mistake! You *have* to change it."

Dad looked taken aback. "Why?"

"It's just terribly affected. 'She sits....He looks.' It's awful!"

"But I wanted to give a certain sense of immediacy," Dad said, clearly rattled. "I wanted——"

"There's never been a good novel written in the present tense and there never will be," Vanessa said, "and that's all there is to it."

There was a pause.

"Also, I just feel terribly jealous!" Vanessa exclaimed suddenly.

Dad smiled.

"I mean, it isn't fair! *I* wanted to be the first one in the family to publish a book...the *only* one."

"I'm sorry, hon," Dad said. "But doesn't it help that it's not poetry?"

"A little," Vanessa conceded. She sat forward, cheeks flushed. "God, it shows what a *terrible* person I am! And what a terrible wife I'd be for Steve! I'm just horribly, horribly competitive.... Wouldn't you feel that way if I'd published before you?"

Dad gazed at her. "Of course not, V....But you're my child; it's different."

"Is it?" Vanessa frowned. "You know, I truly thought you'd never finish it, Dad. I thought we were that kind of a family."

"Which kind?" Mom asked.

"The kind that blathers along, being talented in this and that, but never *doing* anything....I just thought you'd sit forever in your study accumulating nine million index cards and on Thanksgiving when you were ninety, the room would be all filled from top to bottom with index cards and you couldn't even get in the door."

Dad laughed. "I was afraid of that too, V." He sighed. "Hope?"

Mom looked uneasy. "You know, I haven't read that much, like V, so I can't...But the thing is, it's a real book! I mean, it doesn't sound like those amateurish things you see sometimes. It sounds like you knew what you were doing." She took a deep breath. "But there was one thing. This Sophie character? Now, she reminded me a little of someone I know and I just wanted to say—well, I think the Sophie *I* know is a much tougher, meaner, livelier, funnier person than the Sophie in the book."

"Meaner?" Dad said with a smile.

"Yeah, I mean *this* Sophie was kind of a drag, whimpering and whining all the time, leaning on everyone, blaming everyone. I think there's more to her than that."

"Yes," Dad said intensely. "There is."

"You see," Mom said. "The Sophie *I* know is someone who can make it on her own. She wouldn't be desperate without a man. She'd know she could get one if she wanted. She has more—inner strength is I guess what you'd call it. She values love and marriage for their own sake, for the sake of years of shared experience, not because her life wouldn't exist as a single woman."

It was odd. While she was talking, she was looking right at Dad and he was looking right at her. It was as though none of us was there. "I see what you mean," Dad said finally, slowly. "I think you're right."

"Good," she said. Her voice was shaking just a little.

I glanced at Lowell; our eyes locked. He smiled slightly. I wonder if there'll ever be anyone else in the world where I can just look at them, the way I can with Lowell, and know what they're thinking and know they know what I'm thinking. Maybe being married, if you're happily married, is like that.

Y.A. Favorites
from

NORMA KLEIN